1

The Inheritance of Things Past
By
Ben J Dutton

Bob,

For being a good first reader,

Ben J Dutton

Published in 2008 by YouWriteOn.com

Published by YouWriteOn.com

Dedicated To

William Cecil Dutton (1910 – 2003)

and

Ian William Dutton (1965 – 2002)

Thank You for the Inspiration

Prologue
Christmas 1998

'Is it not strange that desire should so many years outlive performance?'
-Poins in William Shakespeare's The Second Part of King Henry the Fourth, II.iv

1.

The mountain stream babbles along like a chorus of flamingos. The grass whispers quietly, a rustling across the open plains. There is the occasional rock strewn like yesterdays garbage, detritus of nature. The sky should be blue, but today it is grey, dull and lifeless. Clouds seep along, ill treacle black, threatening thunder.

You could be at Hiroshima after the bomb, or sitting in the wastelands of the Somme after the fight; the desolation of this place is haunting. You are nowhere, watching and waiting. Your heart beats slowly, in rhythm with the hum of nature. Your mind is wandering; all you can see is the rush of water over pebbles and it seems almost soothing.

Three days ago you made the journey from the city to this place, unsure of what you sought. Now you are here everything seems to make sense.

Once you spent some time in an isolation tank, alone with your thoughts, resting in water. Watching the swirl of psychedelic colours in the contours of your mind allowed you to forget that the bank wanted money off you, that your lover had gone, and that your mother had died a year before. Now you know these things, are aware of their once malignant hold on your emotions, they carry no weight, they are dead, and you can let them go.

Now you are here, you are glad. It was hard finding this place. You had a map, on it the signs of an old deserted monastery and footpaths and towns, but it gave no directions on how to get here, to this place. So you chanced it, a drive from the city and then clambered on board a tired bus, alighted when it felt right, and then walked. You are surprised you ever made it; nobody seems to have been here before. You looked for the signs. A beer can or chocolate wrapper, but all you can see is nature. It is the most unusual thing in the world.

Stretching your fingers out like arrows you lie back on the grass and watch the sunlight locked in battle with the sky. Shards of light break through occasionally then fall back in retreat.

As the first raindrops caress your face you leap and run for cover, but there is none. Frantically you scan the horizon. Life! There must be life! But there is none. Not even the wild chatter of animals in this rock drenched land. Where have you been sleeping? Where have you been hiding? Your life, that's where.

And for a moment you close your eyes, and then you see it.

The doctor has that expression. He has not worn it since last Christmas when he told you your mother was dying.

'How bad?' you ask, already knowing the answer.

'The cancer is spreading.'

'How long?'

'It's not an exact science Will.'

'How long?'

'Soon,' he says, 'soon.'

2.

It is nearing Christmas again. A thousand Santa's parade the streets, swinging bells and illuminating lives. A little girl is recounting her dreams to one outside *Burger King* as I pass, and the little snatch I hear makes me smile: '…Hawaii Barbie, California Barbie, oh and some make up and…' Every lamppost is decorated with tinsel and an icon of the season, Rudolph, the sleigh, Santa, holly, all glowing warmly into the cold evening air. The street is a tableau of rich colour.

My home feels empty. That mornings post is piled up behind the door, mostly bills I realise fanning through them quickly, but slipped in-between two is a pink envelope with a feminine scrawl across it, my name written in blue pen. Dropping the others on the living room cabinet I fall down into a chair and stare at the envelope. It's Laura, we write so often I recognise her scrawl. I can't open her letter. *Laura.* She feels a lifetime ago, though I saw her only yesterday. The way this woman has become so ingrained in my life is everyday a beautiful and surprisingly strange thing.

I hold her letter for a few seconds, contemplating its contents, until dropping it with the bills, knowing I'm not ready to face her. In the kitchen I take two paracetamol to alleviate the headache I feel forming. My life is a mess. Around the work surfaces the remnants of last night's meal fester. A plastic bag and cartons from the Chinese, a dirty plate, and a glass still filled with a little red wine.

I had sat and eaten in silence, while *Who Wants to Be a Millionaire?* carried on mutely in the corner. Even yesterday I had known the news, felt it inside of me, like an eel had penetrated my stomach and was coiling around, frantically trying to free itself.

For a second I feel I'm going to collapse but manage to steady myself. Who to call? Who to call?

I flip on the TV and begin to channel surf. Hundreds of channels and nothing seems to appeal. Then there it is; I almost miss it. Tucked away in some small corner of the digital world, forgotten artefacts for the cinematic archaeologists to find. *Jules Et Jim*. I haven't seen that for… My God, since I was still a teenager. That blonde girl, the one whose name is fogged in my mind, clogged behind the headache, I saw it with her. The film has already started, but I amaze myself by remembering the plot, the details, the feelings it once stirred in me. I can see her now.

Her name was Sarah and she was a philosophy student. She spoke with a light accent that I could never place, and though she was in her early twenties, she acted as if still seventeen. She was flirtatious, gregarious and totally different to me in every way. It was a relationship, I now recalled, based on nothing but sexual attraction. *Jules Et Jim* had not even been her choice of movie, and instead of watching it she insisted on trying 'make-out' on the back row.

As I remember these moments I see Laura's letter again, still unread, on the cabinet where I left it. Discarded waste. How could I have done that? Has this love been stripped of its allure?

The red light is flashing on the answer phone, though I do not remember it being like that when I came home. Hitting the button I hear a hang-up and then David's voice filtering to me through the poor speaker. 'I just got a phone call from Brad Pitt! Yeah, *the* Brad 'hunk' Pitt. He's interested in the Cartwright script. So get your lazy arse over here!'

Work. I haven't thought about work. And that just throws up other things I haven't thought about. Jesus, how does someone deal with getting ready to…? Before I know it David's number is processing away on the autodialer. David is my partner in Riverbank Films, and my oldest friend. If I can talk to anybody it should be him.

'Where the hell are you? Brad Pitt's coming to town today! Like right now!'

'I can't come David. Something's... kinda come up.'

There is a shift in his tone, 'What's wrong??'

I pause a second, imagining the excitement over David's face and wonder for a second if Brad Pitt is *that* actor. His special friend. 'I'll call you later, see how it went. You don't need me.'

'I guess I just turn on the old charm.'

'You'll have him eating out your hand.'

'I wish.' David hangs up before saying goodbye. That is how he is - never say goodbye. Without goodbye, you will see that person again.

I look down at the auto-dialler and see Laura's name. Number 3. I wonder about calling her. There is the letter, we need to talk. But I walk away. I put the woman I wanted to marry at number 3. Wondering who takes up the other two slots, I walk back and look. David and Dad. My father. I *should* call him, but he always seems so distant when we speak. I only have his number on there for emergencies. But this is an emergency my brain howls. I reach to hit the button but back away again. Picking up the car keys I decide to drive.

When I was a child, still young, about four or five, I crashed my father's car. My parents had been fighting about something – I remember not why, but I can imagine it was about money or lack of love or both – and I ran out of the house and onto the driveway and clambered into the front seat of his car. While there, sitting crying, Dad stormed out and I ducked to hide, hitting the handbrake at the same time, and very slowly the car began creeping down the driveway, picking up speed, careering towards a wall. I heard Dad scream and I shot up straight like a rabbit caught in headlights. I fumbled, not knowing what to do, crying, locked tight in one position, until the car crashed into concrete. The damage was only minimal, a scratch on the bumper, but Dad shouted at me like it was the crime of the century and bought his hand down on my behind for what felt like a thousand times. I never got into that car alone again.

The engine of my car hums to life now and I pull out into the street, sliding in behind a black taxicab. As I reach the head of the street, though, I realise I have no direction. That going either way would achieve nothing, and suddenly I have an urge just to get out now, leave the car idling, motor running, going nowhere. Instead I turn left, and head out of the city, up towards Cambridge.

3.

I remember my first trip to Cambridge. I was seven years old and my parents were taking me to see their old college. Dad told me that one day I would be attending university there, that I would follow in his footsteps. There was snow on the ground that day, and I just wanted to be throwing snowballs at Jimmy and Patrick and Pete, not stuck in a car, going to boring-old Cambridge.

I kept telling Dad that I needed to pee, making him stop at all the service stations. It was 1971 and in that maroon, rusted old Ford Cortina, I threw tantrums when he said no and tantrums when he said yes. Anything but to arrive at Cambridge.

I only remember this because of the irony. I loved Cambridge. Until she died, Mum remembered what I said. 'Wow'. That's what I said, and she liked it.

Now I'll be seeing it again for the first time since I graduation. Such a long time ago now. Once there had been too many bad memories for me here. Bad memories no longer seemed to matter.

Sarah had been here.

Now, driving towards Cambridge, I realise that as I get older things get easier and harder all at the same time. That is the way it has always been.

And then a flash of Dr Patel in my mind and another errant thought. This could be one of the last times I drive a car. It's a peculiar thought, and I wonder what other unrealised strangeness festers in me. For a second I just want to keep driving, but eventually, I know, for the pragmatist in me says so, there will be no more roads. Just a cliff and I will be going over.

Two days ago I remember having a conversation with someone. It was somebody important, but I cannot recall who they were or how I met them. They could be man, woman, child, animal, even alien. I just don't know. They told me that if I kept walking out this way I would eventually arrive. Perhaps they were not real at all, but just in my head. The drugs they have me taking now often send me spinning into my cerebellum, cruising on high, feeling like one of Ken Kesey's Jolly Pranksters. Is that even what they were called?

Dulled by painkillers. Will, I want to say to myself, get a grip; it's not the end of the world. Only it might well be. For me, at least. And now I laugh, laugh louder than I've ever felt myself laugh, so loud I think I am disturbing the grass and the rocks and the stream.

Soon, he told me, soon. He repeated it, driving it home, just in case I missed it the first time. Soon I would be dead; soon I would be walking through those pearly gates and shaking Saint Peter by the hand. But what if it all goes wrong and I don't go there, what if I end up in hell or, God, what if it's worse, what if there's nothing?

Is that what he even meant?

Shut up, I shout in my head, and maybe out loud, I really am not sure anymore. Shut up Will, this is it, face it, deal with it, be a man.

The mobile phone in my car rings, once, twice, three times before I answer.

'Will Hargreaves,' I say, speakerphone on.

'Will. It's Rajiv Patel. Are you in your car?'

'I can talk. How are you?'

'Fine thank you. We need you to come in an hour earlier on Wednesday. Does that suit your timetable?'

'That's fine. I'll see you Wednesday.'

I hang up, not wanting any voice intruding in this sanctuary. This reminding me of the reason I hate mobile phones, reminding me that I only got one because Mum was ill and Tia, my sister, or Dad might have needed to get hold of me at a moment's notice. I take my eyes off the road a second to turn the radio on, and car cuts in front of me, forcing me to break suddenly.

The signs indicate Cambridge is getting closer with familiar regularity.

I remember the first time I saw a punt drifting along the waters of the Cam. They were the most confusing, strange craft I had ever seen. Mum put an arm around my shoulders as she knelt beside me and explained some of their history, whilst my father puffed away on his pipe, watching a pair of swans' battle over a slice of bread. As we walked into the city centre I admired the buildings, their elegant form, and wondered why my home town did not look so beautiful. 'Look,' my father spoke, 'that's where your mother and I first met.' He pointed to a small cinema. 'We were both going to see *The Apartment* – you remember that film Eileen? How we laughed and cried.'

'And you held my hand as that girl tried to kill herself.'

'Shirley MacLaine.'

'Yes! That's her.'

I remember being bemused by their talk, it seeming somehow unfamiliar yet natural.

My legs tired as the day wore on, but I could feel something special was happening on this trip. That my parents argued less, that somehow they seemed younger, though I did not know how that could be.

A lorry cuts across my path, blocking the view of the spires of Cambridge appearing in the distance and I feel anger in my gut. I don't want any of this traffic on the motorway, I don't want to see anybody, to feel that anybody else could exist in this world. I want to be left alone, to scream out in rage and sadness and joy.

My mobile phone rings again, shattering the cyclone. 'Will Hargreaves.'

It's David. 'Am I genius or am I genius?'

'I told you, don't get ideas above your station. You'll do yourself an injury.' My repartee feels forced, unnatural.

'Brad 'I'd like to take him up the ass' Pitt...'

'David!'

'Would you say no?' He laughs, mechanical sounding through the speaker phone. 'He said yes! Brad Pitt said yes! He's going to do the Cartwright script.'

'That's fabulous David. Really well done.'

There is a second's silence. David, preternatural, reads my mind. 'Is something up?'

I think about telling him. I really do. 'Not at all.'

'Laura said she hasn't heard from you.'

Can I just hang up? Is that allowed with friends? 'I've been busy.'

'Where are you?'

A falsehood is better than the truth here. 'Stuck in a traffic jam in Kensington.'

David is silent a moment more, mulling this over. 'Well have fun. If you want to talk.'

'I know.' I want to hang up but I seem to carry this conversation on, 'Well done on the Brad Pitt thing.'

'But would you? Come on, tell me you would.'

'Would what?' Now I really want to hang up. This conversation has gone on much longer than I want. Am I doing this deliberately?

'Take him up the ass?'

'Yes David. I would anally bugger Brad Pitt.' My voice is completely deadpan, lifeless.

'I knew it,' and then David hangs up, and I exhale loudly.

I pull into a service station and find a parking space, shut the engine off and close my eyes. They feel heavy all of a sudden, as if I have been awake for days and sleep now needs to drag me under.

Watching a HGV struggle out of the parking lot I feel for the first time tears rolling from my eyes. I wipe the first away, ashamed of my emotion, but I stop when the tide comes stronger. Laying my head down against the steering wheel as the sadness and the fear and the hope - I am surprised by hope - come crashing through my heart and lungs, like the eruption of strings in Elgar's *Cello Concerto*. Part of me wants to call somebody on the telephone but yet another part says just sit here, don't do a thing. Because by doing that this all might go away.

I look up and see a little boy walking hand in hand with his mother across the parking lot and he sees me. I try and smile and give him a little wave. A whole life still in front of him; love and hate, sadness, joy, depression and elation. And I think of Laura, long after our first date, talking about children and how I wanted them. Wanted them with her. A little brother or sister for Natalie, her daughter.

I feel my rational side saying talk to somebody, talk to somebody. Picking up my mobile phone I scroll through the numbers. *Dad, David, Laura, Rajiv, Tia.* Laura. Her name sticks out like a lightening rod and I scroll back to it and look at the digits, knowing them all by heart, the only girl's number I have ever been able to remember. She wants to talk; I see her letter in my mind's eye. It is hard to press the 'dial number' button.

In the cocoon of the car I grip the steering wheel and squeeze my eyes closed, tight, trying to feel some form of pain. A surge of rage, of sheer disgust at everything that's happening to me, that has happened to me and that is going to happen. 'Shit! Shit! Shit!' I shout to nobody, slamming a fist down onto the dashboard, cracking the Perspex that covers the speedometer. 'Shit,' I say again, deflated this time.

And then I start the car and drive the remaining half hour into Cambridge, driving through those familiar city streets. Stopped at traffic lights a gang of young drunken women stagger over the road, laughing and talking loudly, floating on high, joyous and brazen. Full of life.

I am going to stay in a cheap hotel. Not that I cannot afford anything more expensive, but because I do not want to deal with the niceties and faux-kindness of obsequious concierges. I find a suitable place and ten minutes later I am on the bed, fast asleep, dreaming emptily.

PART ONE

CHILDHOOD
1966-1984

1.

Once, when I was in school, I played Tybalt in *Romeo &
Juliet.* I barely remember the performance, but I do remember in
the seconds before I walked onto the stage I forgot all my lines.
Everything just slipped right out of my head, mush crumpled
under foot. I wanted to walk out onto that stage, look at the
audience, and see their expectant gazes widen, and deliver the
performance of my life. I wanted to hear them cheer; to see my
name emblazoned in lights. But I stood on that stage, throat
drying, and off stage the teacher whispered, 'what art thou
among these heartless hinds?'

In my head, now, I wonder why I remember this. Why
anything stirs in my mind, a tender snake coiling around my
subconscious, restless. What all this might mean?

2.

I'm twelve now. It's a family holiday at Black Rock Sands in North Wales, where the sea pounded white sands and the sun beat down from dawn to dusk. I built sandcastles, played chase with my sister and fell in love for the first time. A friend of my sister. A girl by the name of Ellie. Ellie with the smile.

The two of them had gone looking for crabs in some rock pools. I followed, bored, thinking I could play a prank, get them to fall into the water or scare them somehow, but as I pursued them, Ellie turned around and looked right at me and smiled. *And that look.* My heart melted all of a sudden, like ice dropping away, after the rain. I smiled back, dizzy, and she giggled, reached out and pulled my sisters arm and the two of them ran quickly away, enveloped in sun.

I lost her in the sand dunes. At first I didn't mind; the thoughts that had flashed like cannon fire in my subconscious meant nothing because I did not understand them. I thought again, oh that's just a girl and she doesn't matter. But as I leapt about, under that crisp summer sun, I saw her smile at me again

in my mind and I went looking for her. It didn't take long to find
her. Tia and Ellie were taunting a crab with a stick, partially
repulsed at the creature, mostly trying to overcome their fear of
it. Tia was cajoling Ellie into touching it with her finger, and
they were both laughing.

I watched cautiously from the sand dunes, unsure whether to
approach. I knew in that moment Ellie was beautiful, but
looking back on it now I know it was a sweeter, safer love than
now, because it was sexless. Just respect and attraction to who
she was.

'Go on Ellie. I double dare you. Touch it.'

'No!' She squealed as Tia pushed her towards it and once
again they were laughing.

I move closer.

'I'll buy you a choc ice if you touch it.' Tia says.

'One from the shop in town?'

'The expensive ones.'

'I just have to touch it?'

I move closer.

My sister nods, and Ellie, spurred on by the challenge and
possible reward, began inching towards the crab.

'It's dead,' I say, finding some courage inside myself.

The girls jump, startled by my intrusion. 'Go away smelly,'
Tia says.

'How do you know it's dead?' Ellie asks.

'It's not moving. Of course it's dead.' She doesn't seem sure.
'Look, I'll show you.'

Ellie is moved by my sense of nerve and jumps towards the
crab before me. Its pincher click shut and it begins to scurry
away from us. The three of us scream and begin running. Tia
scarpers in a different direction, and Ellie and I both run for what
seems like miles before stopping. Breathless, and laughing.

'That was really brave,' I say to Ellie, for some reason I do
not understand.

'I wanted the choc ice Tia promised me.'

I also know she is lying, not sure how I know these things, and that she was attempting to impress me.

'I'll buy you a choc ice,' uncertain if I have the money on me.

'That's sweet,' and she smiles again.

I look away, embarrassed, and watch an old man with his dog walking along the beach. Turning back to look at Ellie, she moves very quickly and kisses me on the cheek and backs away almost as fast.

'Why did you do that?' I am shocked.

'You didn't like it?' She seems really shaken; her face is going bright red.

I think for a second, realising I do. 'I did.'

Ellie smiles, and moves forward again and I realise she is going to kiss me. I pull backward, suddenly afraid.

'We better find Tia,' I stutter, backing away from her.

Ellie looks confused. I know she wants to say something but she does not.

We walk away from the seclusion of the sand dunes, back onto the beach, where my sister is playing with a stick, drawing letters in the sand. My heart beats so fast I feel it.

These memories of my past are fragments, built more on a foundation of emotion than actual memory. I remember what it felt like in these moments not what actually happened. I wonder if any of it happened the way I remember it. What is memory anyway?

Then.

My mother is asleep in the front seat. Noting this I lean forward, over her, to grab the chocolate bar I can see protruding from her handbag. My father's hand slaps my arm before I reach it. 'You cheeky rascal!' He scolds me, quietly, so as not to wake my mother.

Is this before Ellie or after?

'Sorry Dad,' I say, unsure if I mean it.

'That's for Tia. When we get back home.' I look at my sister, curled up on the backseat, sucking her thumb, lost to Neverland. This is before Ellie. Tia is too small, too young. 'You had yours before we left. Remember?'

'How long until we're home?' I ask, ignoring his remonstration.

'A couple of hours. The main road was blocked. Everyone was asleep so I thought I'd come the scenic route.'

I realise that normally outside the window I would be able to see buildings and lights and people, but that all I can see in the inky night is the shadows of trees and bushes rushing by.

'Have you been here before?' I ask my father.

'I was born around here. While they're sleeping, shall we see?'

I nod enthusiastically, and about twenty minutes later my father pulls into small passing point. 'Come on' he whispers, taking the torch from the glove compartment as surreptitiously as he can manage, and the two of us gently close the car doors before walking into the countryside. I'm not sure what time it is but it feels late and exciting, because in my mind it is dangerous, forbidden.

My father darts the torch light around, revealing warped tree trunks that look almost alive, towering deformed creatures trying to eat me. My imagination sparks, a huge grin crossing my face in the eternal blackness of night. Off somewhere I hear the hoot of an owl and expect to be afraid, but expectation keeps the fear at bay, and I feel myself tread confidently beside my father as he navigates this open path.

We are climbing up a hill, I can feel the tiredness invading my legs, but I do not grumble, for I realise that this is a special moment, that to say the wrong thing now might shatter the uniqueness of it all. How I know this I'm unsure, but I do, and that is all that matters.

'When I was a young man,' my father begins, 'before I met your mother, I used to know a woman by the name of Josie. She was a lovely girl, bright red hair, had such a sweet laugh. I can still hear her laugh now. We used to come walking up here together, hand in hand, and we had picnics on top of the hill. She'd bring bread and cheese and I'd have a bottle of cider.' My father seems to laugh faintly. His story is strange to me. This is not a father speaking to his son, but a confessional. I am honoured to be listening to him. 'I remember I stole the first bottle from the Welshman – what did we call him? – Dai Evans. Dai Evans.' He repeats the name a second time in some strange accent, that in memory now I know is his approximation of Welsh. 'I haven't thought about any of this for years.' He laughs again to himself. 'He told me about a beach in Wales, I remember that. He always said Josie and I should visit it when we had children.'

'Can we go there Dad?'

My father shines the torch in my direction. 'I'd almost forgotten you were there William.' He rubs my head with his free hand. 'You want to go to Wales?'

'To the beach.'

'Dai Evans' beach? Sure, we could do that. Would you like that better than visiting stuffy old Cambridge again?'

'I liked Cambridge.'

My father stops walking and looks down at me. His face is cast in moonlight, looking withered but still ruggedly handsome. I know he is smiling when he asks me, 'You really liked Cambridge?'

'Yeah.'

'I love Cambridge. Your mother's not too keen anymore. It was good to be there today, met some good mates.'

'The Lilywhite players?'

'My old team.' His voice is wistful, then suddenly angered. 'Damn my knee, I still damn it today.'

'You hurt your knee?'

'We were playing Ipswich. I got a foul tackle, knocked my knee out of place. After that more than an hour on the pitch and

I was in agony. I'll hate that player until the day I die. I was going for the big time. Had an offer, go professional. That's what you have to remember Will. Sometimes life throws you a curveball and you have to play it, even if you don't want to.'

My father starts walking again, the torch light pointed directly ahead. I stand frozen for a moment, two, with the cold biting into the skin around my nose and around my ears. Then, as the light of his torch begins to fade I run to catch him up.

My father has stopped. He has the torch pointing out towards the horizon, and I consider telling him to point the torch lower, that he will disturb people who live close by, but when I reach the top of the hill I realise that it would be a pointless thing to do. Outstretched before us is a canvas of night-shrouded countryside, stretching for miles until, off in the distance, I see the glimmering of a town; possibly Cambridge, but I am unsure. The lights glint upward to the moon, a stunning contrast of luminosity.

'It looks beautiful, doesn't it William?' My father kneels down beside me and slings his right arm around me, pulling me in close. 'It's even more beautiful in daylight. I wish you could see this in the daylight.'

'Is that Cambridge?'

'That could be anywhere. That's what's so great about a place like this. Anything can be anything. That town could be Camelot; it could be London, or Marrakech, or Saint Petersburg. There could be a thousand people down there, living their lives, or there could be none. Imagine it Will, right now there are all those people, and they're all doing something different. Some are happy, joyous, saddened, crying, sleeping, having...' His voice trails off, and I know he was going to say something naughty, but has restrained himself mid-flow.

I look up at him and though it is night I can see his face as clearly as if the sun were shining onto it. 'I love you Dad.' I say it, but I don't know why. His smile is ashen; I know the colour has drained from his cheeks, though I cannot see this.

'I've made some mistakes William, but you forgive me, don't you?'

'Yes.' Again I do not understand what it is he is trying to say, but this time he realises it and rubs my head and kisses me on the forehead.

'Let's get back to the car. Mummy might be wondering where we are.'

He begins to walk back down the hill, his torchlight held low, playing against the grass. 'Daddy,' I say out loud, not knowing why.

'Yes son?'

'Did you love Josie?'

My father stops, turns back to face me, and walks back to where I am standing. 'Yes. I did. Not as much as I love mummy, or you or Tia, but I loved her. Do you know what love is, then?'

I think for a moment. 'It's when a man rubs noses with a woman.'

My father lets out a snort, and then a roaring laugh that saturates the hills, sends a cuckoo into a nervous fit of cooing, and wakes my mother as she sits in the car, breaking the silence of her dreams. He laughs louder, pulls me into a bear hug, and I feel his warmth surround me.

After a while we are driving again. The road narrows out, becoming a dirt track. In the front seat of the car my mother stirs, perhaps awakened by the rising tension in my father's breathing.

'Where are we?' She asks, sleepily.

'Er…' my father stammers, 'somewhere between Cambridge and home.' He tries to be flippant about the situation, but that only increases the panic my mother has felt since waking.

'Are we lost Daddy?' Tia asks, innocently. I did not even know she was awake.

'No, no. Just taking the scenic route.' Mum scowls at him. 'OK, we're lost. I've been trying to turn around, but this road is too narrow. If we just keep driving, we're sure to find a main road soon.'

'You always do this Geoff.'

'Don't start snapping at me. It's not my fault.'

'You took this route just so you could go off gallivanting on the hills at night. Don't think I don't know about you Geoff Hargreaves.'

'And what's that supposed to mean?'

'And this route, you've only taken it because you don't want to go home. I know all about it.'

'Stop fighting,' I shout. Next to me, Tia is trying to hold back her tears.

Mum turns around, 'we're not fighting, honey,' she taps my leg and throws a comforting look at Tia. 'You better get us home soon,' my mother hisses as she turns back around.

'Keep your Barnet on,' he jokes again.

Mum mutters something under her breath; something I now know would have been curse words.

I look out of the window, trying to take my attention away from their fighting. Outside the car the hedgerow is menacing as it speeds past, shadow figures leap out at me, and the unreality of it sends chills down my back, a pool of sweat forming in the small of my back. The hillside seems an eon ago, another journey.

And then there is a sharp jolt as the car lurches forward, howling in pain, and a boom and the car shudders, shakes, I feel my heartbeat caught in my throat, and the car comes rolling to stop.

'What the fuck's happening?' my mother shouts. 'Oh shit, sorry. You didn't hear Mummy say that kids.' Back to my father, 'What just happened?' Her voice is stained in fear.

'I think something's blown. A fuel-line maybe. I'll go look.'

He gets out of the car and as he flips the bonnet open a rush of black smoke hits his face, and he backs away quickly. 'I think you better get out,' he says.

Tia starts crying, shaking in her seat. Mum is shaking too, but she manages to get out of the vehicle and comes around to Tia's side and lifts her out of the car. I get out too, and walk around to the front of the car, and watch as the smoke rises up into the night sky. 'Is the car on fire, Daddy?' Tia asks.

'No, no it's not.' He waits a minute for the smoke to clear and then walks up to the car again. The three of us remain huddled together beside the hedgerow. My imagination spins me around, expecting to see a bogeyman coming out of the gloom.

'I think the diff might be stripped.' He says.

'What's that mean?' My mother asks.

'It means... it means we're stuck here. I can't fix this.'

'You've got to. There's no chance in hell that I'm sleeping out in the middle of nowhere with you tonight.'

'We're stuck wherever we go,' my father mumbles softly, I barely catch it. He slams the bonnet down. 'I'll go look for a house. Somebody's has to live around here.'

Dad begins to walk up the track. 'Don't go Daddy,' Tia shouts after him.

He walks over to her, 'I won't be long honey. Ten minutes, that's all. You've got Mummy here, and William. He'll look after you.' I remember a strange sensation of pride when he said that.

'Well go if you're going,' my mother spits. 'Let's go sit in the car children.' She marches Tia over to the car, and I follow, wondering whether I can actually go with my father instead. 'We can get in the car? It's safe?'

'Yeah,' Dad says as he begins to walk down the track, his hands buried in his coat pockets, head hung low, buried under his flat cap.

'Daddy!' I shout after him.

'What?'

'I love you.' I don't know why I say those words to him then.

He looks at me; I know he doesn't know how to react, whether to come to me and hug me, or whether to say those words back. As he stands there, I realise for the first time what those three words mean, that there is a depth to those words. They cut right into you.

'Get in the car with your mother,' he finally says, and then carries on along the track, disappearing into the darkness.

It is my father pounding on the window of the car that wakes us. He looks pale, and I unlock the car door for him.

'You finally came back then,' my mother chides. 'Thought you'd run off to Timbuktu.'

He ignores her, 'I found a house. Eventually. They've called a breakdown service; it's on its way from Cambridge. The farmer gave me this.' He hands a small package into the car and my mother opens it. Inside I see a thermos flask, some biscuits and bread. 'It was all he had. He'll be down to help us out once he's milked the cows. We're on his road, that's why nobody's been past.'

Mum gently taps Tia on the shoulder, waking her. 'Here you go honey, drink some of this.' She pours some milk into the cup and hands it to Tia who swallows the liquid quickly.

'Well. At least you can't say I don't ever give you adventure,' my father jokes, but getting no response from my mother he turns his back on the car and stretches. I ignore them as best I can, and eat my biscuits in silence.

'Where are we Mummy?' Tia asks, blinking sleep from her eyes.

'I don't know. But we'll be home later, and then you can go play with Jessie and Paula. Would you like that?' Tia nods her head vigorously.

'What can I do Mum?'

'Whatever you want to.' She hisses.

'You can come down the garage with me, if you want. See if we can't fix this car,' my father says. Instinctively I know that my father wants me to agree to this plan, for his main passion is working on the car, but I do not share his love.

'Yeah,' I fake enthusiasm. 'Can I get chocolate for helping you?'

'The biggest bar we can find.'

'Mummy, why does William get chocolate and I don't?'

Mum looks right at Dad, 'Because your father always makes promises he won't keep.' Then she hugs Tia, 'I'll buy you some chocolate, don't you worry.'

Tia smiles broadly, crumbs of biscuit falling from her lips.

Dad grumbles to himself and walks off a little way up the path. I look at him, standing in the brightness of the rising sun, his corduroy trousers not quite the right fit on him, and his cap still covering his head, it all becoming the one iconic image of him. An image I remember with startling fondness.

The swirling, bright yellow light of the breakdown truck scorches my retinas. The driver, in dirty blue overalls, fag end drooped in between his lips is talking to my father. 'It's gonna cost. A big job. We need to get you back to the garage.' His voice has a slight northern pitch.

'Is the car going to be off the road long?'

The repair man bites the fag end and looks over the car, his head at a crooked angle. He hums, seems to be making a few mental calculations, and then pronounces, 'A couple of days, no more. I said it's a big job, but we can do it right. And quickly for you.'

'Will someone drive us home?' Mum is worried.

'Yeah, no probs. We'll sort all that out for you. Just sign your life away here,' he lets out a chesty laugh, then coughs deeply, his cigarette butt somehow managing to stay in place. 'Thank you my good man, thank you. Now let's get this thing moving again.' He walks over to his truck, winking at Tia as he goes, and she cuddles in behind me, hiding away. The man begins his complicated procedure of hooking our car up to his truck. 'We'll have you out of here in time for a late breakfast.' The man laughs deeply again, but this time I don't see any joke.

3.

The leafy street we called home resounded with the laughter of my friends, their Sunday game of cricket already underway. I felt pangs of disappointment as I stepped out of the rescue truck, I should have been third batsman today.

'We called for you,' little Tommy from number seven shouts. 'Where you been all day?'

'Go play,' my father pushes me towards my friends.

Not wanting to question anything now, not after the night we had, not after the things I saw and the things I heard said. I run towards the cricket game with false enthusiasm.

'Our car broke down in the middle of nowhere,' I babble. 'We were there all night. It was really scary. We could hear things moving in the bushes, and Dad had gone off to find help and we thought he could be dead.' My friends listened to my tall tale with the right amount of interest and doubt. As the story finished I realised quite a crowd had gathered around me, and in amongst all my friends was a new face.

'Who are you?' I ask the stranger.

'This is David.' Tommy explains, 'he's just moved into Barry's old house.'

'Hi David,' I say, 'I'm Will.'

'Hi,' David says, smiling. I think he's a little shy, maybe a little reserved, but I like him instantly.

I follow my friends into the woods. Tommy is carrying a stick that he is brandishing like a spear, and is pretending to stalk and hunt our imaginary Indians. David walks beside me, at a slower pace than my other friends up in front. I keep in step with him.

'Tommy said you went to Cambridge yesterday, with your Mum and Dad.'

'They used to go to university there. Dad thinks I'll go one day.'

'My Dad wants me to go there too. He keeps saying. You don't want to go?'

'No. I'll be playing for Everton. Striker.'

As I talk with David I think about some of the things that happened during the night with my parents, about why they are fighting so much these days. They never used to, and their behaviour is disturbing me.

'Can we go to the sweetshop,' Tommy shouts back to us, 'I wanna buy some crisps.'

'Whatever you want,' I shout back to him, and then to David I ask, 'do you have any pocket money?'

'No. I don't think my parents thought about it, they're too busy unpacking.'

'I can lend you some, if you want?'

David thanks me, and the three of us cut through the undergrowth, fighting through the brambles and the ferns so we can climb over the fence onto the main road. Overhead the sun is pounding the earth, and for those few moments clambering through the bushes I am glad to be out of the heat.

In the shop we bought two packets of crisps and two Mars bars, and then the three of us retreated back into the woods where we sat around and greedily munched on our treats. Tommy carried that look of devilish glee, as if our actions were forbidden.

'Do they have a cinema around here?' David asks.

'There's one in town. You have to catch the bus.'

'They've got this new movie called *Jaws*. It sounds scary. Do you wanna go? My dad will drive us; he wants to see it too.'

'What's it about?'

'A killer shark.'

David kept building the suspense until an hour later we were in David's home, pleading to see this film. The thunderous opening bars of the theme music electrified our bodies, plunging us into another world. Cinema consumed us both that night.

We emerge from the flickering darkness and night has fallen.

'That was so brilliant!' David exclaims.

'I've never seen anything like it. One day, you and I are going to make a film like that. Killer sharks.'

'I got a better one than that. We can do anything. Killer dinosaurs. In a city or something.'

'A t-rex running after a car. Wow, that'd be so cool.'

'Before you kids have a fit, I think I should get you home.' David's father says, and ushers us towards his parked car. 'Your mother said you're to be home by nine, so we have to go straight there.'

'Can't I stay at yours? David and I have a film to plan.'

'Not tonight. Maybe next weekend.' David's mother says.

As David's parents talk, the two of us run towards the car, and I am unsure whether I hear his mother say, 'it seems like David's found a new best friend.'

David's parents watch from their car as I walk the stone pathway up to my front door. I kneel down and take the door key from under the flowerpot where my parents have always left it for me. Looking back at my friend, David waves, as do his parents, and I know I'm going to like having him around. I unlock the front door to my home, the bright light hitting my eyes like a sucker punch, and as they adjust I see Tia sitting on the stairs, arms around her legs, trying not to cry.

'What is it Tia?' I ask, closing the front door.

'Mummy and Daddy are fighting again!'

Somewhere, in the back of the house, I hear something smash against a wall, the sound of glass breaking echoing down the hallway, and my mother shouting, 'Don't you give a fuck? Tia's probably out there crying and William is on his way back.'

'You don't listen to me!' I hear my father shout back.

I am about to run through to them, to scream at them to stop fighting, when my mother comes storming down the hallway, tears streaking her cheeks, her skin reddened. 'Come on kids, we're going to Granny's. Daddy doesn't want to be with us anymore,' she grabs me by the shoulder and tries to lead me towards the door.

'What's Daddy done?' Tia asks, 'I don't want to leave Daddy.' She dodges Mum's hands, and runs over to our father and throws her arms around his waist.

'Go with your mother, sweetie,' he says, trying to free himself of her grip.

Tia holds on tighter, though. 'What's going on, why are you fighting?'

'Because your father's been a lying, cheating pig.'

'You don't need to bring the children into this Eileen. It's not their problem.'

Mum scowls at Dad, and I see her reaching for a vase that is on the side cabinet, but she stops when she feels me hug her tighter. 'Why did you do it?' She says instead, anger, resentment and pleading in her voice.

'I don't know.'

'You must know. You don't just fuck some other woman for no reason. For seven fucking months!' She rages, pushing free of us and charging at my father.

'I love you Eileen, not her.'

Mum stops, looks at him, suddenly bewildered. I look at my sister, she is shaking, and then at the faces of our parents that seem alien to us at this moment. I grab Tia by the hand and lead her into the living room, as my parents stare at each other across the hollowness between them.

'What's Daddy done?' Tia whispers to me, between her cries.

'I don't really know. Don't worry, they'll sort it out.'

As I close the living room door behind us, I go to turn on the television to drown out their fighting, but I hear Mum say, 'how can you love me, and still fuck that little tramp?' Before I hear his answer, though, the television springs to life, and I sit Tia down in front of the set, and collapse beside her, trying to ignore the emotions fuming through my skin.

Tia has her head resting against my shoulder, the glow from the television now turned to snow, reflecting light onto my face, my tears glistening in the half-light, when Mum pushes open the door and smiles at me gently, sympathetically.

'Daddy and I have stopped fighting now. We're sorry.'

Dad appears beside her, an arm around her waist. 'Parents just have to fight sometimes, sometimes about stupid things. We just forget how to talk.' Dad looks at his wife and kisses her on the cheek. 'It's time you went to bed kiddo.' He walks into the room and picks up Tia, who stirs in his arms, yawns, but returns to sleep.

Mum walks over and turns the television off, the room sinking into shadows. She comes over to me and sits down. 'You should never worry about us darling,' she says, and squeezes my shoulder. 'This won't happen again. Daddy will talk to me again before giving me a reason to shout at him.'

I look at her for a moment, not sure what to say to her, 'Can I have a glass of warm milk?'

'Sure,' she smiles, 'let's go to the kitchen.'

Then the memories of youth fade. They become contended, peaceful days, the days of unspoiled delight. The years roll quickly by. It seems over night I went from ten to twenty. There are images, flashes of things. The kiss outside *Ray's*, with Gwen, my first real kiss, running, and jumping and singing and the euphoria, the so so strong emotion that overwhelmed me when the Cambridge admission letter arrived on our doormat. I was leaving home, leaving Abingdon far behind. Going forward. To another life. The second phase of my existence.

It is the love I remember. It is to those I have loved my memory walks me, a hindsight guide, who shows me I have been blessed, never mind what comes next. What comes next?

'How soon?'
'Soon,' he says, 'Soon.'

Are you even sure anymore? Of what has been said to you, of what is important? What in this language of yours means anything?

You are still here, in desolation, watching. Though now you see more, are aware of more life, more potential for life. In this breathing of the grass there are whole ecosystems, exosystems. You are here but you are not here. Molecules of dust and light, molecules of life contorting and expanding about you, a million thousand explosions a millisecond and the hum of life is invisible, indivisible to you.

You close your eyes to this natural life again, seeking out from within the darkness the face of your other, Laura.

Laura. What to say about Laura?

She is smiling at you now. Her lips widen, the white of her teeth showing. Her blue eyes blink at you, you in reverence of her. She is more than anybody else. And yet her image fades, slips away, receding into that darkness. You call her; call her by name, screaming in your subconscious and in the real world. You call her name, over and over, louder and louder. You are

43

running now, running for your life, running towards her,
through the expanse of life.

But there is still more to dream. To live. To remember.
What is in the inheritance of things past?

PART TWO

UNIVERSITY DAYS

1984 - 1987

1.

The First Autumn

I see her in yellow. Yellow t-shirt, black trousers and her
blonde hair long and flowing. She smiles at me as I pass. She
has no name. I have never seen her before, but in that impetuous
way I have, I feel it is real, forever, and meant to be. So I go to
her, sitting on the wall with her friends, and say, 'hi,' and she
blushes, looks away, and then returns the greeting. The awkward
pause of what to say next begins to form between us, festering.
'I was wondering if you could help me,' I begin to make up
words on the spot, my head feeling like a swirling pool of water
in which I am drowning. 'I'm looking for the finance office.' I
seem to like drowning before her.
 The sun is shining through the trees, an orange glow filtered
through green leaves, the light flitting across her face,
illuminating her eyes, deep and blue. 'The finance office?' she
asks, and stands, 'I'll show you,' she continues, smiling a smile

of white teeth and ruby lips that I so want to be kissing, 'I'm dreadful at giving directions.'

As I walk besides her, looking at the ground, searching my brain for something to say, I realise how tall she is. She's my height, and though I'm not exactly a giant, it's a thought, and for a moment I feel like blurting it out, just to have something to say.

She breaks the silence. 'Is this your first term here?'

'No, not at all. I've been here a year already.'

'And you don't know where the finance office is?'

Ah, I think, caught out. What if I am wrong? What if her smile was not an expression of attraction? I stop walking, and look straight at her. 'I'll be honest. I don't need to find the finance office. I know full well where it is. I just wanted to, I don't know, talk to you.' I look away again, feeling tiny. 'I just sort of wanted to know you. Sounds crazy, I know.' She is silent, her look not deviating from me. Feeling smaller still. 'Look, let's start this again. My name's...'

'Will. I know who you are. I'm Sarah. And this has to be the oddest chat up I've ever experienced.'

'How am I doing?'

'Pretty pathetically, but I like your fumbling. It's charming,' she laughs. 'Feel like getting a coffee? There's a nice place down by the Cam. It's quiet.'

Sarah seems to be leading me away from the Cam. I realised it about five minutes ago but I haven't said anything, instead I'm listening to her talking about her degree. I am in that moment when conversation seems almost impossible as no questions seem to form, and when they do they seem to be the most idiotic – what kind of music do you like? What kind of films? Have you been abroad? What's your favourite cheese? Admittedly, with hindsight, I would know that not all of them were stupid, and little would I realise I would ask them all anyway, as time passed by.

Suddenly she stops, 'This is my place. I've just got to get something.' She opens a small wrought, rusted iron gate, and begins walking up the short path. 'Come in,' she opens her door and I follow her in. Her house is a small semi-detached, typical student bed sit, the smell of cigarettes circulating like bad air freshener, and I see two girls and number of boys sitting on the floor of the front room. 'Those are some of my flatmates and other assorted layabouts.'

She carries on walking by when one of the girls comes out. 'Hey Sarah, is that gig today?'

'You know it is.'

The friend suddenly realises I am standing there, 'well hello,' she says in the most casual voice she can muster.

'Will meet Egg. Egg, Will.'

'Egg?'

'I got attacked by an egg once.'

I look at Sarah, the bemusement obvious. They both laughed. 'It's a long story that's sort of not.'

'Like that, hey?'

'Something like, yeah,' Egg giggled. 'Well, I'll let you get on Sarah. Will.' She smiled a second at me and returned to her other friends.

'So what's this gig?' I ask, again looking for conversation.

'You'll see.'

'I'm coming, am I?'

'You will do. When you see what it is.' She started up the stairs. 'Hang there, I'll be right back.' She disappeared into a room halfway up the stairs, emerging a minute later.

It is a flash in my heart. I definitely want to go.

The cafeteria was pretty chic. Great décor, way ahead of its time, lots of tables sitting facing the small stage. Every table was already taken. Sarah asked me to sit at the bar, and she slipped out back with her guitar. She was here to sing. This is what she did on her downtime. Sung live in cafeterias and at parties and at festivals and even on the streets.

The barman asked me what I was having, compliments of the house, so I ordered a beer – *Fosters* - somehow I recall even that little detail. As he poured I saw Egg and the others slip quietly into the bar. Egg saw me and waved and they all came over.

'So she dragged you here. Must mean she likes you.' Egg just came out with it.

'How do you figure that?'

'You're the first man she's invited to see her play. How long have you known her? She's not mentioned you before?'

'About an hour.'

'Really. Wow. Hope you're a good guy. Sarah's been burnt a lot, wouldn't want you to do the same.'

Something clicked in my mind, like the shutter of a camera coming off. This was how they did it, how girls operated. Told you they like you then sounded you out through their friends. The easy way to gather information. To prepare themselves for the first moments of intimacy.

Sarah has changed her clothes. She is wearing a loose fitting top, the colour of deep red wine, and black trousers. It suddenly feels like it's ten at night and not early afternoon. Her face framed by candlelight and the low glow of a spotlight. She is carrying an acoustic guitar, and into the microphone she says hello, that her name is Sarah Crowe, and that this is a song she wrote last night. A few low strums on her guitar, and then the melody shimmers out of the strings, gentle, rhythmic, and then she sings, eyes closed, touching the void.

Her voice was exquisite. I watched her as she floated high, her voice iridescent, and her left foot tapping gently on the floor.

'She's beautiful, isn't she?' Egg breaks my reverie.

'Yeah she is.' I say without even realising it.

'Do you even know I'm sitting here with you?'

I turn and look at Egg. 'I think I was in my own little world then.'

'I'll say. Let me guess, Sarah was in every scene.' I'm not sure whether I'm blushing. 'Do you know, I never believed in love at first sight, but I see you looking at her and I doubt myself.'

'You think I love her?'

'I think you love an idea of her right now. Let me guess, you always wanted to date a singer?'

'Actresses, actually. I'm a movie fanatic.'

Egg mused on this a second then said, 'Sarah and I went to see that new one the other day. What was it? *Paris, Texas*. It made no sense.'

'It's Wim Wenders. It's sort of the point with him. What did Sarah think of it?' I ask, casting a glance at her, retuning her guitar.

'She liked it, I think. I was sort of stoned after the fact.'

'Does she..?'

'Take drugs? No. She's a good solid girl. You don't have anything to worry about with her.'

I knew that Egg was eulogising Sarah purposively, but I didn't mind. All I cared about was the fact that it meant that Sarah liked me. Why else would her friend be so enquiring?

Then Sarah let out a few more notes from her guitar and began singing again. I turned my back a little on Egg letting her know I wanted to listen to nothing but the music once more. Sarah winked at me before she started to sing, and my heart glowed.

Sarah finishes her set and half an hour later she is with me at the bar. I can tell she has retouched her makeup and hair, and she looks lovelier than before she went on stage. Egg's comments shoot through my mind, feeling like truisms.

'You were very good.'

She blushes, 'thank you,' and she looks away, embarrassed.

Where there was once music and sound now stands the pregnant silence. Sarah looks at me, then away. I try and think of something to say to her, but nothing that I have experienced so far in life has prepared me for this moment. I contemplate saying that, but it sounds facile. She touches her hair and takes a sip of her orange juice.

That simple movement provides an avenue of conversation, 'You don't drink?'

'Not when I'm on a gig. It gets in the way. I don't feel I can perform.'

'I can understand that. It's interesting, though, that you say that, because often people say they can't perform without alcohol in them.'

Sarah looks straight at me, a gentle smile crossing her lips, and she laughs suddenly, unexpectedly. I wonder what she is laughing at, then I realise why.

'I didn't mean...'

In a playful, flirtatious voice she asks, 'Do you need alcohol to perform? Is that why you've been sitting here drinking *Fosters*?'

'No. No. I mean... I don't know what I mean.' I laugh, perhaps out of nerves more than anything else.

As I feel my cheeks redden, Egg reappears to save further embarrassment. 'That was a real hot gig Sarah, you were on fire.'

'Thanks,' she says impassively, and I am aware that this girl wants to be alone with me.

'Everyone says so.' Egg carries on regardless. 'The manager loved you, he wants you back next week, says he has an evening of live music planned.'

'That sounds great for you,' I say, trying to say anything.

'It does.' Sarah thinks for a moment. 'I'll talk to the manager later.'

'He wants to see you now, says he needs to talk about contracts.'

'If he's that desperate for me he can wait a while.'

'That's it, he can't. He's seeing a band down in Bognor tonight, then he's up to Glasgow for three days. He needs to organise this before he leaves.'

Sarah looks right at me, and rubs her foot against my leg for a second, two. 'I need to go do this.'

'You go; I'll be here when you get back.'

'You're a sweetheart,' she says, and kisses me on the cheek. 'Danny,' she grabs the barman's attention, 'Give this man another pint. He needs the alcohol to perform.' She laughs and squeezes my shoulder before disappearing into the crowds, lost in vapour.

I was aware that it had gotten dark outside the bar. I watched as the shadows increased against the back wall, only to be illuminated by electric lights. Sarah had been off with the manager of the bar for well over two hours, during which time I had elected to stay, not sure where or when I could get to see her again should I have left. The barman had been some conversation, talking about his love for motor racing and football, whilst I tried not to reveal my ache to love and my ache for Sarah.

It was 9.43 on the clock when she reappeared, somehow that time searing itself into my memory with such clarity that I can still see the clock today. I remember being infuriated that she had been gone so long, but also the sheer pleasure that she had returned. She did not look at me straight away, not even aware that I was in the bar any longer, until I waved and her face widened with joy, forcing the tired look from her eyes.

She ambles over, still oozing sex appeal, with Egg standing someway behind.

'You stayed.' It sounded like a question more than a statement.

'I did, yes. I didn't feel like saying goodnight when we did.'

'We could have been a lot longer. The owner wouldn't shut up. Egg and I stayed until it no longer felt impolite to say we had to leave.'

'So three and half hours is that time.'

'Has it only been that long?' She laughed gently. 'It felt about six and half.'

'Well I've had this wonderful bar to keep me company.'

'You're not drunk, are you?'

'No. Two pints, that's all. I didn't want to act the fool when you came back out.'

'What would you have done?'

'I don't know. Probably tried to kiss you.'

'You need to be drunk to kiss me?' She slid her hands onto my legs and moved in close to me, her lips closer.

'I guess not,' I say as she kisses me. The best kiss ever.

Their house had been transformed. The remaining housemates had been busy adorning the front with balloons and banners. It was clearly someone's birthday.

'It's Rob's. He's one of the guys that shares with us. That's why only Egg stayed down the bar with you, the rest had to organise this. Do you fancy helping us celebrate?'

'If it's not an intrusion. I don't know Rob.'

'I'll introduce you. You'll love him. Come on.' She grabs my arm giving me no other choice, and drags me into the hallway. Everyone seems gathered in the same room I saw them in before, still drinking wine but now apparently playing a game.

Sarah leads me in and introduces me to the eight people sitting around, but I make no effort to try and remember their names as I know I'll have forgotten them all by morning.

'We're playing the truth game,' explains one of Sarah's friends. 'Ever played that Will?'

'What are the rules?'

'I'll make a statement, like 'I've never slept with a donkey',' a few people giggle, 'and if I have I stand up and drink a shot of this whiskey. If I haven't, I stay sitting and don't get anything.'

I nod, the juvenile nature of this game not appealing, but I see Sarah is wishing to join in, so I take the seat next to her on the couch.

'You start us off Will.' Sarah forces me right into it.

'Come on Will. The dirtier the better,' the same friend that explained the rules says.

'Ok. I've never…'

'You have to stand up to speak.'

I exhale, run a hand through my hair and stand up. Looking down at Sarah I think for a moment and she smiles back at me, urging me on. 'OK. I got one. I've never slept with anyone on the first date.'

There are a few groans, 'everyone's done that,' someone says, and before I know it the whole room is standing and the whiskey is being passed around. Sarah takes a swig from the bottle and passes it to me.

'If I've not done it, I don't drink?' I ask for explanation. Sarah nods. 'Then I can't drink.' I say.

'How very noble of you,' Egg giggles. 'I think you've caught a gentleman Sarah.'

Sarah squeezes my hand, and I pass the bottle to the next person.

As the game continues the level of drunkenness in the room increases, until through slightly blurred eyes I brazenly throw an arm around Sarah and she nestles into me. Then the bottle arrives again at Sarah, and freeing herself from my arm, stands up.

She looks at me, straight at me, and says, 'I've never wanted to sleep with anyone in this room so much as I do right now,' and she takes a very long drink from the whiskey bottle, and passes it to me. I look at her, the alcohol fogging my brain, not sure whether I am hearing what she is saying right, but I finish off the bottle. Sarah smiles, stupidly, strangely, and then pulls me up off the sofa and drags me towards the door.

'Don't keep us up all night,' someone, possibly Egg, shouts, and I hear the raucous laughter as we climb the stairs to Sarah's bedroom.

It is as I expected it to look. On her wall are pictures of musicians and other teen idols. In one corner of the room a pile of dirty laundry, and on her desk various books, a half written essay and sheet music. On her bed, which I notice has actually been made (and I wonder whether she cleaned up when she disappeared for five minutes earlier in the night), and a teddy bear sits between the pillows.

'Take your shoes off,' she says, 'sit down.'

She kicks her shoes into the corner of the room. Going over to her record player she puts on a James Taylor LP and then lies down on her bed. I place my shoes by the door and then lay down next to her. The whiskey is still swilling around my head. I pick up the teddy, 'so who's this?'

Sarah gives me another stupid drunken grin, and takes the bear from me. 'This is Daisy. My grandpa gave her to me when I was five. She's my oldest possession.'

'And you take her everywhere now?'

'She's my good luck charm. Do you have anything like that?'

'I don't know. I don't think so.'

'That's sad. You must have something?'

'I don't think men do. Not the ones I know, at least.'

As I talk I can feel my body accepting the alcohol, Sarah's face becoming clearer. I look at her skin, closely, and see the light application of makeup around her eyes and her cheeks. She looks at me quizzically. 'What is it?' She asks, rolling onto her side so the two of us are now facing each other.

'You really are beautiful,' I say.

She places her hand onto my face and pulls me closer. The kiss is powerful; I feel my lungs being ripped out. Her hand slides down my body and between my legs. I put my hands up

56

her shirt and undo the bra clasp, fumbling at first, and then finding the right way. Sarah leans up a little and pulls her shirt off and throws the bra away. I look at her breasts, kiss each one tenderly. 'I wanna fuck you,' she says.

She darts across the room and switches the light off, forcing the room into an eerie orange glow cast from the streetlight outside. Shadows swing across the ceiling when a car passes by, and whilst the hum and laughter of the party continues downstairs, I connect with this woman in a way I thought impossible, blood firing pistons in my heart and mind, her skin smelling of lavender.

Sarah kisses my chest intermittently as she rests against my naked body. Her fingers stroke my stomach and my sex. I run my fingers through her hair and kiss her on her forehead. Sweat glistens there, a pearl.

'That was amazing Will.'

I kiss her forehead again at the compliment.

'It was great. You were great.'

She pulls me in close, my skin tender against hers.

'Do you mind if I stay the night?'

She looks up at me with her blue eyes, and then she licks up my chest, to my mouth and kisses me hard, her tongue entering my mouth. When the kiss finishes, she smiles, 'I want to wake up next to you Will Hargreaves. I want to taste you in the morning.'

Her words sound honest, but I cannot believe that this beautiful young woman is saying them to me.

'Is that a yes, then?'

She kisses me on the cheek, 'of course that's a yes.'

I kiss her on her neck, moving slowly down towards her breasts, down her belly, between her legs, down her right leg and kiss her on her feet and suck one of her toes. My confidence sexually is surprising, but I try not to think about it, just go with the flow.

'You wanna go again?' She asks as I stand up and look down at her, naked on her bed. She slides down towards me, onto her knees in front of me and takes my sex into her mouth. For a moment I wonder what has happened to the music that was playing on her turntable when this started, but realise the music probably ended a long while before. I shudder as new sensations ripple up my spine, and I rest a hand on her head, unsure where to put my arms.

Sarah releases me, detecting my insecurity and stands up, kisses me on the lips, and swings a leg around my leg. 'We'll do anything you want to,' she says.

I have not had sex like this before. Nothing matters; it is more than just sex, this is emotion and raw passion. All consuming. I grab one of her buttocks in my hand, and crush the air between our bodies, as we fall back down onto the bed.

'Do you like domination games?' Sarah asks, overconfident.

'I don't know,' I reply, perhaps a little too honestly.

'I do. Will you let me dominate you?' She bites my ear playfully.

'I don't know. I've never really done this before.' I think of her on the stage, singing those songs earlier – she was earthly, sensual, tender. The questions she is now asking seem to be coming from a different person. 'What do you want to do?'

'I want you to be my slave.'

'And do what?'

She pulls away from me a little, inflating the space. 'You're not being very cooperative Will.'

'I just don't know what you're asking of me. You didn't ask for this earlier, what's changed?'

'Nothing. I'm… I'm overcompensating.'

It's not what I expected her to say. 'Overcompensating?'

'I'm afraid to ask things.'

I can feel realisation dawning. She can ask things of me in a game, but not when it something she actually desires and does

58

not wish me to know of, in case the truth embarrasses her. I almost want to speak my insight out loud, but I do not.

'What do you want me to do...? Mistress Sarah.' I want to laugh, but I do not.

A huge smile of relief crosses her lips, and she once again pulls in closer to me, her hand rubbing my sex for a minute, lust coursing my veins. 'Go to the end of the bed and kiss my feet.' I kiss her on the lips and obey her command, seeing how difficult it was to for her to ask. As I lick her left foot she trembles, closes her eyes, and my desire for her increases.

On the bedside table a candle flickers out, plunging the room into night.

Sarah is cuddled in next to me, one of her fingers tracing outlines of invisible things on my chest. I look down at her, and play with a strand of her blonde hair.

'I never asked you,' I begin, as she kisses my chest gently, 'when I met you this morning, you knew who I was. How?'

She kisses my chest again, 'You showed me around. On the open day.'

I recall that day, but not Sarah.

'Didn't think you'd remember. I was pretty quiet. Stayed at the back. I remembered you, though. I thought you were cute.'

'I'm honoured.' I touch her forehead with my lips, and she pulls me in closer to her. 'So what are we doing tomorrow?'

The two of us carry on talking into the early hours of the morning, and somewhere, I don't know when, sleep caught us both, dragging us away, her legs entwined with mine and her breath on my lips, caressing me as the moon drifts on by.

***

I'd heard in song of people saying that when someone was on their mind, that wherever they went that person went with them. I'd never believed it, but for that first week whenever I wasn't with her, all I could see was Sarah. When I dreamed she was there, a beautiful woman seducing my dreams. I'm not sure what I missed during that time, for although I still went to lectures, still read for my essays, lived the academic life, none of it seemed truly to sink in. It was just Sarah, Sarah, Sarah. And of course when we met up, spent a night together, or a long evening, it just heightened everything, made it all hyper-real. After a while I wasn't even sure how I'd coped without her before. I even started doodling her name, like some romantic schoolboy.

"It's that serious, is it?" Liz, one of the girls who shared three lectures a week with me asked some point into the second week.

I looked down at the book into which I was supposed to be taking notes and again saw Sarah's initials scribbled there.

"What are you? Still ten?"

Liz had been a good friend, the first person I met on my course. She put me to shame, always focussed on her work.

"Who is this goddess that has you so transfixed?"

"Sarah Crowe. God she's beautiful Liz. I think I might be..." I was going to say in love, but stopped short, wondered why I was telling Liz this, and not Sarah.

"As someone once sang, he's got it bad and that ain't good. I hope she treats you well Will. You don't deserve anything else."

After class I took a walk along the Cam, thinking again about Sarah, imagining the possible futures we could have together, remembering the power of that first night together, remembering the feelings she aroused in me; those strange, wonderfully new feelings. I am in love with. I am in love with Sarah Crowe.

2.

The First Summer

In the last week of the academic year I asked Sarah to come
home with me. Falling into my arms we kissed, and she
accepted this mad proposal.

We spent the next few closed off days in her room, shagging,
sleeping and planning. We both needed work, desperate as we
now were for cash. 'I can sing,' Sarah said, 'places are always
looking for a night's entertainment.' I told her about a bar near
my home that booked singers. There was the worry we'd left it
all too late. Dad called me back the next morning and said he'd
got Sarah two bookings, but that was it. Twenty quid for the
two, spread over a month and a half. It wasn't a lot, but it was
something. At the start of the first week of the summer holidays
we found ourselves in Dad's caravan at the end of the drive,
broke and desperate.

'I can't let you stay rent free,' he told me, 'and I know you haven't any money. So,' he passed Sarah and me a list, 'these jobs need doing.'

Clean the guttering. Paint the spare room. 'That's my room.' I told him.

'And you're an independent man now. You should be in your own place, far from here, earning a fortune to send back to your Mother and me.'

After he left Sarah laughed, 'Is he always so bossy?'

Tia was in her last year of school that year, and Abingdon being the quiet town it was then – is now – she and her friends had little to do. Just to get out of the house she came and sat in the caravan at night and played card games with us. Sometimes some of her friends came over or we all caught the bus into Oxford and watched some film at the cinema. The fifteen weeks of that summer seemed to career into the distance, no visible end in sight. After what felt like one month the calendar reprimanded us with just the one week crossed off.

'Are you sure this is the best way we can spend our summer?' Sarah asked me one morning, as it rained outside, and we huddled under the duvet covers, an electric fire going. 'I mean, it's June and we've the heating on and we're broke.'

'And we've a house to paint.' I reminded her, partially joking.

'We should be doing something. Egg's off travelling Italy. I could have gone.'

'Your parents are tighter than mine. I know this isn't the romantic life, but if we want to spend this summer together it's the sacrifice we have to make.'

We saved up some money and had our occasional days out. We caught the train to London and met up with some friends, went wandering through the museums taking in fine art. We had some laughs, some jokes, shared a bottle of wine and two, and for a few hours felt that we weren't trapped in my father's caravan. Then we returned to our temporary home and the long extending days seemed to taunt us.

After a while we stopped Tia from coming over so regularly. It seemed strange that we should be spending our time with a group of teenage boys and girls.

Then at the start of August – how we got to August I do not know – David, my best friend, returned from Paris where he had been living.

'I want to be a bohemian.' He had written to me before he left. 'I want to be a left banker, meet Godard and fuck Leaud.'

He knocked on the door of the caravan at eight in the morning carrying a bottle of wine, wearing the white flares he seemed to have been wearing since '77, a crushed velvet shirt, silver jewellery around his neck, a beret on his head and the darkest, largest pair of shades I'd ever seen.

'Did they forget to tell you glam died?' Sarah asked from the bed.

I was resolutely aware that my girlfriend was naked in the bed and my best friend had just entered the caravan uninvited. I was glad she at least had her sense of humour.

'Well hello.' David dropped the bag he was carrying and lowering his head so as not to bang into the roof, leapt over the accumulated junk that littered our floor, and proffered his hand to Sarah. Her hand came out from under the duvet and taking her hand in his, David kissed it. 'I'm David. I'm sure Will's told you all about me.'

'Unless he's been collecting gay friends called David, then yes, I know all about you.'

David shot a glance back my way. 'If such a beautiful lady wasn't in his bed, then I might just believe he's been collecting gay men. After all, he's had such a penchant for me for so long, haven't you dear?' David stepped back over the junk and embraced me, kissing me on both cheeks, his hand squeezing my buttocks. 'So you two have been at it like rabbits, judging by this firmness.'

'You are filthy David Roper.'

'Just how you like me.' He smiled. 'Got a corkscrew in this mess? It's time to celebrate.' He set the wine bottle down on the table and collapsed into one of the seats. 'Don't mind me. I've just been dumped.'

I gave him the keys to the house, told him to go inside and sort himself out, and then returned to Sarah who was already getting dressed.

'Are all your friends so invasive?'

'Just David. I don't think he knows any boundaries. I'm sorry. I'll say something to him.'

'You better. I don't want him thinking he's staying in here with us.'

'I'm sure he's going home.'

'You don't invade someone's home with all your belongings if you're going home.'

I looked at David's bag – packed tightly, large. 'That's probably just his clothes for today.' I tried joking. Sarah gave me such a withering look I decided not to make any more.

She moved over to the sink and started filling the kettle. 'Does he drink tea or coffee? Or is it just wine?'

Her bad mood made me feel uncomfortable. 'I'll take David to the cafe in town; find out what's going on. Tell him he can't stay.'

'Good. Because I'm not sure I want to see him here again.'

'You don't even know him.'

'And already I don't like him. He thinks he's charming, that the camp routine gets him off anything. I don't trust him Will, and I don't think you should.'

Not wanting an argument this early in the morning I kissed Sarah quickly and went to leave the caravan.

'Will?'

I turned around in the doorway.

'This is our home, and it's tiny. It can't take an ego like his. I'll be happy to see him in the pub, or whatever, but not here. I was naked and he just barged in here. I know he's gay and that this,' she indicated her body, 'that this means nothing to him. But it's still invasive. The duvet might not have been on or anything. Just don't invite him back here. Please.'

I agreed, grudgingly. I could see how she might find David overwhelming, and maybe I was biased because I had seen this man shaped out of the boy he was. David was just David. David always did as David wanted to do. And that never mattered before.

'I'm going shopping with Tia today,' Sarah carried on. 'We won't be back until late.'

I closed the door to the caravan and met David coming out the front door of my parent's home, carrying a plate with scones and tea on. 'I forgot how smashing your Mum is Will. If she keeps feeding me this well she'll make me the king of the lardies. Where's Sarah?'

'Inside. Getting dressed.' I indicated that he take a seat by the outside table. 'Finish that then we're going into town, find a cafe, so I can have breakfast.'

'I'm sure your Mum will cook something. I saw her making Geoff a bacon butty.'

'We're going to town David. And that's that.'

We walked down the streets that had once resounded with the chants and cries of our long cricket games. The street that was our pitch was busier now, more cars, speed bumps, but the echo of that time was still there. I could still see David running after the ball, running, running so fast his legs seemed to blur, chasing that six I hit, when the ball rolled right down the street, right into the hands of Mr. Clark from number nineteen, who snatched it right up and said he'd return it to our parents and have a word about our playing on the street. 'Could smash a window.' He chided, 'Or hit someone in the face. Do some damage. You should all know better.'

I smiled at the memory. Then asked David, 'Whatever happened to all the kids we once knew? I don't see any of them here anymore.'

'Last one I heard about was Johnson. Remember?'

'Is he still in prison?'

'Might be out now. I'm not sure. Shouldn't be let out if you ask me.'

Johnson had attacked an old lady whose house he had broken into, attacked her with a metal pipe, left her for dead. It was an intrusive memory. Not one I wanted resurrecting. But I could see him now, the little boy with the temper even then. When we were kids.

I changed the memory. 'Whatever happened to George? You had such a crush on him.'

'I did not!' David laughed. 'There was only ever one boy I had the hots for.' David swung out, putting his arm around my neck and drawing me in close. 'But he only ever liked the beautiful women.' He rubbed his hand on my head, knuckles into my skull, then released me. We carried on walking. 'So come on lover boy. Tell me about her. I know you're itching too. You always took great pleasure in tormenting me with the stories of your love conquests.'

'I do not.'

'What was that girl's name? Ellie. You went on about her for weeks. Ellie from the beach. Ellie with the blonde hair. Ellie the kisser. Then there was Jennifer in year eight. Kate, Sophie and Gwen in year nine. I lost count in year ten. And now you're shacked up with an absolute goddess.'

David reached into his back pocket and removed a pack of Marlboro cigarettes. Lit one up and passed it to me, then lit another for himself.

'I gave up.' I told him.

'Fuck off.'

I started to smoke. 'I met her at uni.'

'I figured that. There was never any girl that hot in this town. If there had been I'd never have gotten a chance to know you. You'd be off sniffing their skirts.'

I laughed. 'Do you know what David? You do look a twat.'

'What?' He stopped, turned to face me full on, striking a pose. Like he was on Top of the Pops.

'I don't know how this town ever coped with you.'

'I don't know how it's coped without me.'

'How was Paris?'

'Fuck off again. That reminds me. How is she in bed?'

'Now it's your turn to fuck off David.'

We started walking again; taking drags on our cigarettes, and looking at the facades of houses we once knew the interiors of. It felt so long since our childhoods, even if they had only just ended.

'Do you remember the names of all my girlfriends?' I asked David as we reached the end of the street.

'Only the ones that kept you from me sweetie.'

We walk in silence for a while, looking around, watching, and waiting.

Then I realise what I haven't asked. 'Who was he?'

David sighs, 'Only the love of my life. Guilleme. Gill, as I called him. Sweet ass. Great ass. We fucked all over Paris and I let myself fall in love. God. Nothing seemed to matter when I was with him. Fuck I miss him Will. I really fucking miss him. I found him in bed with another. You know how it goes. We all know how it goes. Fucking hell. But we never see it. Do we? Fucking Gill and his magnificent cock. God that cock tasted good. But he got *it*. Didn't he just. Fucking got *it*. Fucking stupid bastard. I'm not sure how you can love when there's that. *It*. Why do we let ourselves fall in love? She'll do the same. You're beautiful Sarah. They all do. In the end. I'm not even sure there is something called love anymore. I think we just fuck for a while and then... fuck it I'm done. Over. *Finito*. That's it.

No more boys. Just men. Old men. Because at least they're a little more desperate to hold on to you.'

I cut into his rant. 'You'll no more go for old men than Sarah will cheat on me.'

'I'm sorry. Of course. I shouldn't have said that.'

'Don't worry David. She doesn't like you either.'

'Well thank God. Because I wasn't looking forward to faking it for the rest of the summer. I don't mean to cruel Will, but I have to say this. All *that*, that's why I know it won't last with you two. I don't like her. Your family can't like her much either. Why else would they put her in the caravan and not in the house?'

'Because they've turned my room into an office already.'

'Bullshit and you know it. And if none of us like her, then eventually you won't either. I'm sorry old chap. But I guess we all have to learn it sooner or later. I learnt it will Gill. You'll learn it with Sarah. Love fucks you up and it fucks you over.'

I looked at the pavement, at the green grass cutting up around one of the trees, breaking through the grey. A thousand thoughts seemed to be vying for space in my subconscious. I focussed on David's words, and then looked up at him only to see him looking away, into the far distance. We stood there, on that street corner, in the early morning sun, as a group of children in the back of their parent's car pointed at David and giggled. How incongruous he looked in this suburban Oxfordshire town.

'You should be in Hollywood.' I said to him.

'I'm thinking about going.' He admitted and then threw his arms around me, his head falling onto my shoulder. His body heaved with the first tears of the day.

The cafe in the town centre was already filled with morning shoppers, and a group of workmen in reflective jackets either coming off or going to work, or both. They were noisy, laughing and joking with one another. Not for a second did we think of looking for somewhere else to eat. *Ray's* was our place; where we always came, where we grew up. From its windows we had watched the pretty girls (and in David's case the pretty boys, though in secret for the first few years). Always on his tape deck Ray would play fifties rock and roll. I remember coming back with David from Oxford having just seen *American Graffiti*. *Ray's* became our movie diner. Outside its doors I had my second kiss, my first proper kiss, with Gwen from year nine, my first kiss with tongues. David pulled funny faces in the window. I remember being so nervous, remember wishing that I was back inside with David, talking about Harrison Ford in *Star Wars*, play acting Han Solo. Gwen got pregnant when she was fifteen and moved to Basingstoke. In my mind the two were connected. If you got pregnant you went to Basingstoke. It put me off going there for such a long time. The idea of all those pregnant teenage women put me right off.

'The terrible twosome. Back in town. How're you lads?' Ray came out from the back to say hello. We exchanged pleasantries, and he took our order personally, and said he'd get right on it. It was good seeing him again. At least some things remained the same.

'So tell me about Sarah?' David asked after Ray had dropped off two steaming mugs of tea.

I told him the story of how we had met, of the last year we had spent together. He listened intently, asked very few questions. He allowed me to spiral off in my reverie of her. 'You should hear her sing David. The most amazing voice. She's already got a booking for next year's folk festival in Devon. It's a big thing. She's going to be huge.'

'And you figure in these visions of greatness, do you?'

Of course I told him yes. Yes I do.

Mum and Dad let David spend the first night he was back on their sofa. He stayed in the house with them and watched soap operas while I waited for Sarah to come home. When Tia reappeared without Sarah I asked where she was.

Tia explained, 'She wanted to go to some boring art gallery. So I came home.'

When she failed to reappear after twelve I thought about calling the police station. Instead I walked down to the bus stop in town and looked around, but saw only youths hanging about there. I walked back to my parent's home just as a taxi cab carrying her pulled up. She fell out of the back door, shouted something back to the driver and tossed some money in. I ran over, picked her up and collected the money, handed it to the driver who said, 'she's your trouble now, she is.' And he drove off, leaving us standing in the street, in the pale moonlight.

'Where the hell have you been?' I demanded as I carried her back towards the caravan.

'At some party in Oxford. Didn't realise the time. Why?'

I didn't have the heart for a fight so I remained quiet, until we got to the caravan and she started screaming.

'Why are we here?! We shouldn't be in some shitty caravan. I want a decent bed, a decent night's sleep. I'm going home Will. I'm going home.'

'It's past midnight.' I tried remaining calm.

'You just don't fucking get it, do you! Do you?'

The light went on in Tia's room and I saw her peering though the crack in the curtains. Sarah was still screaming, so I pushed her into the caravan, pushed her onto the bed and slammed the door shut behind us.

'You'll wake the whole neighbourhood Sarah. Have some consideration.'

'Come on Will. Grow some backbone. Argue back. Stop being... nice. You're too bloody *nice*.' She spat the word. It sounded a foul, vulgar word on her lips.

She got up off the bed and came to me. Her eyes were drunk and fiery. Unexpectedly her lips were now on mine, biting at me, vicious towards me. She held my shirt, pulled at it, spun us around and threw me backward, onto the bed. Her fingers clawed at my trousers, at my shirt.

'Come on Will.' She hissed, 'Some fucking backbone!'

Her fingers, scissor-sharp, sliced my shirt away, sliced my skin. My chest bubbled in sharp pain. She came atop me.

'Come on Will. Fuck me hard. Fuck me to wake the neighbours.'

A wild beast, she pushed my boundaries, pushed us to the stratosphere. The caravan howled.

'God you were loud last night.' David took me to one side the next morning. 'I wouldn't take her into see your parents. They were so embarrassed. We were still up, playing Trivial Pursuit. What did she do? Let a rabid cat loose in there with you?'

Flushed with embarrassment myself, I bit my lower lip, took the tray with our morning tea on back out to the caravan. I avoided the eyes of my family. In the caravan Sarah was packing.

'I don't want to lose you Will,' she said, 'but if we stay locked up in here together we're going to lose one another. We need more space.'

'I can't be without you Sarah. It's still another six weeks until term begins.'

'I'm not proposing we be apart Will. I'm proposing we go back to Cambridge right now. My landlord said we might be able to move back in early. If not we can crash with friends. I spoke to Mum; she's willing to sub me the rent for a month. But I can't be living here, with your parents, in this caravan. We need space to breathe; and more solid walls so your Dad doesn't look at me like I'm some tramp.'

I knew there was no counter argument I could make. Sarah, as always, had made her mind up.

I felt guilty about leaving David in his heartbreak, 'I'll be fine old boy.' He tried putting a brave face on. I knew he was scared to hell of being left in Abingdon on his own. 'Besides, Hollywood keeps calling. I've still got *some* money.'

Two days later we were at the house in Cambridge, back in the bed we first shared together, in an otherwise empty house.

At least until Egg returned, the following morning.

'I heard you were back.' Egg said. I didn't want to ask who off. I already knew Sarah had called her. That Sarah could not stand the two of us alone in this house. A week later I got my own flat. And then we were normal again. Best friends, together almost all the time, with the best sex. There was just space. If we needed, or wanted, it.

The new academic year began and I got a postcard from David. 'In Hollywood. Met a guy. I'm in love already. He's the best. XXX'

The interregnum of the summer was over. Life was, at long last, back on track.

***

"How was your summer?" It is Liz, one of my oldest friends at Cambridge. She looks a little different, more confident, as if the summer break has recharged her batteries, given her a renewal of energy. She has her mousy brown hair tied back in a pony tail. She is carrying an Antonia White novel under her arm, *Frost in May*, I notice.

"It was..." I think about telling the lie I have told everybody else, the lie I agreed with Sarah. The lie that we spent the holiday travelling Europe, that it was all good, and not that horrible reality, of the fights and the near-breakup and the ignominy of returning here early. But this is Liz and for some reason I feel she deserves more. "It wasn't great."

"Oh." She looks for a moment deflated, and then looks up at me with an enquiring smile. "So you and Sarah..?"

"We're still together."

"Oh."

"Just about. We had a rough summer. I wasn't sure we were going to last. But I'm sure you don't want to hear about my problems. So what about you? Do anything exciting?"

Liz shrugs her shoulder; she seems to be closing in on herself, somehow embarrassed.

"Meet any cute guys?"

"There's only one guy I like." Liz blushes.

"Whoever he is, he's a lucky guy to have someone like you interested."

"You really think so?"

"Of course. I wouldn't say if..."

Egg appears beside me. "Sarah won't be long. She's just buying some new picks in the music shop." Egg turns to face Liz. "Hi I'm Egg."

"Liz Walker." Liz offers her hand in friendship.

But Egg takes my arm and turns me away from Liz. "Come on you. Let's go find your fuckbuddy."

"She's my girlfriend Egg. Not some casual fling."

"Whatever." Egg mutters. "Nice to meet you Liz."

Before Liz can respond Egg has pulled us away.

"That was rude." I tell her.

Egg remains silent, and I know she does not care – that she has no time for me – but I am grateful for it. I have no wish to know her either.

3.

The Summer After

It is quiet as I walk along the Cam, the early morning mist still floating casually upon the water. There is the distant hum of traffic, but it seems unconnected to the place I am in. In the sky, breaking the early rays of sunlight are wisps of cloud and the occasional trail of an aeroplane, shooting off to someplace exotic.

I feel the twist of excitement in the pit of my stomach, and I wonder whether Sarah is ready, knowing that she won't be. I know there are things that they will have forgotten to do – fill the van with petrol, buy some food and drink for the trip – that all Sarah will have thought about is the right clothes and to make sure that she has everything for her guitar. For that, though, I cannot fault her. At least in pursuit of her career she is fastidious.

A schedule has been drawn up in advance, but I know too that this will be abandoned, or altered. That I will probably be doing all the driving, as Sarah and Egg and whoever else they invite along will be playing childish games and giggling while I concentrate on the road, and on the things to do with Sarah whilst we are there. That is if Egg and the rest give the promised alone time.

I need the time, that's what ultimately this is about. I think about the last few weeks with her. About the niggling doubts, about that fight I had over some long forgotten point. On the path in front of me an elderly looking gentleman walks with a Scottie dog running circles around his feet. As I pass him I say good morning, and he is taken aback, but returns the greeting and I feel he wants to say why does nobody say good morning to one another anymore? Why does it all have to be so lonely? I want to give an answer but I do not know it.

I feel guilty about pressing the doorbell to Sarah's flat. It is still early, and despite the commotions I know are going on inside this flat, I realise there could still be other residents asleep. Sarah answers the door, pushing my fears aside, wearing a loose fitting top that does nothing to accentuate her form, and a pair of jeans. I kiss her quickly, almost absently on the lips.

'Good morning sweet, you ready to rock 'n' roll?' She asks me as I follow her into the house.

'I am, yeah. Are you guys?' I smell the after burn of incense and marijuana. 'Egg been at it again?'

'Bit of a party last night. Egg's still suffering.'

'Let's get the stuff in the van.' I pick up her guitar case. 'Did you remember to fill this monster up?'

'Shit, no. Sorry, I forgot. You know what I'm like.'

I try and laugh but there is something between us both, like a silent hunter, circling our words.

It takes a good twenty minutes to fill Sarah's vintage camper van. It rusts around the edges, gleaming in the early sun like gold dust. I have a vague suspicion that this journey might end up with the van breaking down and I make a promise to myself not to take them on the scenic route. Once everything is loaded I climb into the driver's seat awaiting departure, only to be grounded for another fifteen minutes as Sarah and Egg make sure that they have packed everything they need and that they are indeed ready to depart. I am glad nobody else is coming.

Once they are both in the van, both on the backseat, I turn and look at them. 'Is that everything now?' I am aware of sarcasm in my voice but cannot control it. 'Nothing else we need? Kitchen sink? More people?'

'Just drive you fool,' Egg retorts, 'we've got a long day ahead of us and we don't need your bitching.'

I turn away from them but catch Sarah's eye in the rear-view mirror. She gives me a light smile and then looks away. I start the van, its engine coughing bronchially, and then it stutters into life. Checking the mirrors before I pull out I have a flash of something old, something ancient stirring in my subconscious. Then before long we are on the road to Cornwall, the travelling show.

I hear the hum of the motorway long before I see it. The roar of traffic, the loud blare of a car horn and the dark rumblings of trucks. 'Now are you sure you know the way?' Egg asks, quietly, so as not to wake Sarah who is now soundly asleep, head lolled back against a small pillow.

I dislike Egg's doubt. 'Of course I do. I spent all last night looking over the maps. Don't you worry, I'll get us there.'

'It's not that I question your ability Will, but just that you are a man, and men aren't too well known for their map reading abilities.'

'Jesus, do you really believe that feminist crap?'

'It's not crap Will. And you know it. If you could just stop thinking with your dick for a while you'd realise it.'

I wish it was Egg that was sound asleep, and not Sarah. At least with her the conversation is far more pleasant. I try and change the subject.

'So why's she sleepy today? Were the two of you up all night lambasting men?'

'I don't know,' Egg replies defensively. 'I'm not with her twenty four hours a day.'

'Is something wrong Egg? You're not normally this… this aggressive.'

She sighed, shook her head and rubbed her eyes. 'I'm just tired Will. We did have a long night and I think I need some sleep. Wake us when we're near Devon.' And with that she turned her head away from me so she was looking out of the passenger window. I glanced at Sarah quickly in the rear view mirror, still sleeping, thought about how beautiful she was, and tried to ignore the worm gnawing at my gut.

Both Sarah and Egg are sleeping now. The traffic on the motorway has thinned out and I am alone with my thoughts. I glance back at Sarah for a second, a beam of sunlight playing against her eyelids and lips. In my memory I see her as I saw her for the first time, sitting on that wall, all that time ago. I wonder what she thinks of me now, in those quiet times when I'm not around – do I enter her thoughts as much as she has been entering mine? Or does she think of others or of nothing at all? I wish I could read her in her eyes when she looks at me, that those blue eyes of hers could become transparent to me. Then I smile and focus on the road once more, overtaking a true Sunday driver and hope it's not long until we arrive in Devon.

Sarah wakes first. I imagine she feels the encroaching sense of anticipation. I left the motorway an hour ago, and we are now weaving our way through the Devon countryside. Sarah stirs, pushes her arms out, trying to stretch. 'Where are we?' She asks, tiredness invading her words.

'Somewhere in Devon. I don't think it's far to the campsite now. Have a good sleep?'

'You should have woken one of us. We said we'd take turns in driving.'

'You looked so peaceful sleeping. I didn't have the heart to wake you.'

'You're a good boyfriend Will Hargreaves.' She leans over the driver's seat and kisses my cheek.

Glancing at Egg, then back at Sarah, I feel like saying something, but I force the words back down.

'How long has Egg been out?'

'Not long after we left Cambridge. It's been peaceful. I've enjoyed the driving.'

Sarah reaches forward again and squeezes my shoulder. 'It's really great that you're doing this for me.'

'And miss the chance to be with you? I just need you to tell me about...'

'Look, there's the sign,' Sarah breaks in.

I glance where she is pointing. There is a bright yellow sign, with black writing on it. '*The South Devon Folk Music Festival.*'

'This is going to be so good. They say last year six bands got signed up.'

'You'll be one this year. I've got faith in you.'

'I'm glad someone has. Jesus my nerves are already going.' She closes her hands over her mouth and exhales loudly. 'This better go well. It's the one chance I've got to hit the big time.'

As she talks, I see the entrance to the festival and turn onto the dirt track. 'This is rural Devon.'

Before us stretch hills, sun-swept and green. Further down the field we are crossing are numerous tents, vehicles and caravans. Just beyond them stands a small stage, speakers mounted under tarpaulin sheets. Sarah nudges Egg on the arm. 'We're here,' she says to her friend, 'we're really here.'

Once the engine is off I see a man wearing a name tag approach. He looks official, young, and handsome. I can see he thinks he's important. He tapped on the window. 'Can I see your tickets?'

I remove the tickets from the glove box, and he looks them over, then into the back of the van. 'I'm Marley, welcome. So which one of you lovely ladies is Sarah Crowe?' Sarah waves at him. 'I thought you might be.'

'Why?'

'You have the look. I'm excited about your set; I've heard only good things.'

'You've heard of me?' She asks, disbelief in her voice.

'There are a few guys from Cambridge here. They heard you play *The Cam*.'

Sarah looks at me, 'I took you to a gig there,' she says, and smiles. 'Thank you Marley.'

'A pleasure. No doubt I shall see you all tonight. Enjoy your stay.' Marley walks away.

'He seemed nice.' Sarah says a moment later. 'I can't believe people already know who I am.'

'I said you were good.'

'Maybe I just like hearing you say it,' she laughs, leans forward and kisses me on the cheek.

'Let's get the tents up,' I say, and step out of the van, into the chilled Devon air. Sarah puts an arm around my waist, and nestles her head on my shoulder. 'Thank you,' she says, and we both stand there for a moment, the silence gnawing between us.

Sarah clutches my hand tightly. Her guitar is resting against the wall as we watch from the wings an act performing. Their numbers are fast, the lead singer's voice sounding ever so slightly out of tune.

'I don't think this lot will get signed,' Sarah murmurs into my ear. 'Even Egg can sing better than him, and she only sings in the shower.'

'Don't get mean now. Just because everyone has said you're good doesn't mean you still don't have to prove yourself.'

She smiles at me and bites my ear, kissing my neck. 'I've got a surprise for you in tonight's set.'

'Oh yeah? I'll look forward to it. I'd rather a surprise after the set, though.'

'I've already got that one taken care of.'

'Really?'

'Egg's coming to do a striptease for you.' She laughs, slightly too loudly, and the bass player shoots us a dirty look.

'I'll look forward to that one. I always wonder what she looks like naked.'

Sarah slaps me gently on the arm, 'I bet you imagine the two of us together, don't you? I bet you get off on it.'

'All the time. It's my favourite fantasy after Margaret Thatcher in a bikini.'

Sarah screws her face up, 'You are a sick puppy Will Hargreaves,' and she kisses me on the lips as outside the crowd roar and applaud loudly as the band finish their set. 'I think it's time for me to perform.'

'Are you sure you don't need any alcohol?' I joke.

Sarah kisses me on the mouth. 'That's your problem mate, not mine.'

Sarah reaches for her guitar as Marley emerges from the shadows and runs onto the stage. 'Next up,' he says into the microphone, 'is a wonderfully talented, gorgeous young singer from Cambridge. We know you're going to love her, and be buying her records soon. It's the beautiful... Sarah Crowe.'

Sarah kisses me again quickly on the cheek and walks out onto the stage, guitar strapped around her neck, and she whispers into the microphone, the spotlight casting her body in golden light, 'this one's for Will.' She winks at me.

As Sarah finishes her set, Marley comes rushing back out onto the stage and touches her arm, then hugs her in tight, and into the microphone speaks, 'Wasn't she wonderful! Let's hear you all appreciate this wonderful singer!' In the darkness in front of the stage I hear the sound of hundreds of people cheering my girlfriend. I feel happiness for her, but at the same time suspicion and anger, I want to charge the stage and free her from Marley's grip.

The two of them stand on the stage for a few moments before Marley says, 'and the next act is the Brown Kettles!' and then he leads Sarah towards me. I feel three large men push past us, carrying their instruments, and they congratulate Sarah.

'You were really great,' I hug Sarah, deliberately getting between her and Marley. 'I liked the new songs, they were beautiful.'

She smiles, and kisses me quickly on the lips. 'I'm on fire after that, can we go get a drink or something?'

'I'll take you to the performers bar,' Marley cuts in, and sliding an arm around Sarah begins to lead her towards the stairs off the stage. Sarah allows herself to be cradled by him for a second, and then looking at me she pulls herself free.

Sarah takes the seat between Marley and me, and slides one hand down onto my leg.

'You were excellent tonight Sarah,' Marley begins, 'I know some people that want to talk to you about recording contracts already.'

'Oh my God, really?' There is a giddy excitement to her voice, and she turns on her seat a little to face Marley, her hand easing off my leg.

'I don't joke about these things. If your friend is alright staying here, we could go talk to some of them now.'

'That would be great. You don't mind, do you Will?'

'Don't mind me, I'm just a groupie.' I try and joke, attempting to keep bitterness from my voice.

'You're an angel,' Sarah kisses me on the cheek and stands with Marley.

'Clive,' Marley shouts to the barman, 'give this man a few on the house,' and the barman nods and comes walking down towards me. 'We'll be back shortly,' Marley looks at me, smiles, and then leads Sarah out of the marquee.

'What can I get you sir?'

'A shotgun.' The barman looks at me, and I shake my head, trying to force the malignant thoughts away. 'Double vodka,' I say.

'Don't mind Marley, he's harmless,' the barman seems to read my thoughts, so I turn away from him, only to see Egg walking into the bar. She waves, and comes across.

'Where'd Sarah go?'

'Off with Marley to talk record deals.'

Egg looks at me, 'You're not getting jealous, are you? Just because another man fancies her right now. She won't do anything, she loves you too much.'

'And how do you know?'

'I'm her best friend. I know everything she gets up too. Sarah knows how to take care of herself.'

The barman places my order on the bar, and I down it in one shot. 'You want a beer Egg?' She nods. 'Two beers.' Egg takes the seat next to me, where Sarah had been sitting just moments before. 'So tell me Egg, what happened last night? I know something did, the two of you evaded the subject all morning.'

'Nothing happened.'

'At all?'

'It's not for me to say. It's Sarah's responsibility to tell you if she does something or doesn't do something.'

'So something did happen last night?'

'I didn't say that.'

'Egg, tell me.'

'Somebody tried it on with her.'

'Who?'

'Just some prick one of our flatmates bought back for the party. He was some first year student.'

'And Sarah told him where to go?'

'Of course she did. Sarah's a loyal girl. You shouldn't even need to question that.'

'I don't. Why didn't she tell me about it, though?'

Egg takes a long drink of her beer, and then looks straight at me. 'She should be telling you this, not me.'

I look at her, at the red flushing into her cheeks, and the way her eyes keep glancing at the floor, trying not to connect with mine. 'Did she sleep with him?' I swallow while asking, my throat suddenly feeling dry.

'I don't think so.'

'I don't think so or you know they didn't?'

Egg grimaces, bites her lip. 'I don't think so. They were in her room for about half an hour. That's all.'

'So she kissed him?'

'She was very drunk.'

'It's no excuse.'

'And high. We took some pot last night.'

'Sarah doesn't do drugs.'

'She did last night'

'So you're turning the woman I love into a cheating drug addict.'

'God you can get so melodramatic. She took a little pot and kissed some bloke.'

'And that's alright, is it?'

'You're fighting with the wrong person Will. I'm not her guardian. She can fuck who she wants to fuck as far as I'm concerned. I don't give a shit.'

'What the hell? Who are you to say these things?'

'I wish she had fucked that guy last night, so you could be out of the picture.'

'You'd like that, would you? Who are you to dictate who she's with? I love her. I'd do anything for her.'

'I know. She knows it too. That's why she kicked that guy out last night. That's why she stays with you all the time. It's a real kick for her, having someone worship her so much. It makes her blind to everything else.'

'What's that mean?'

'Like you give a shit.'

'I've been nothing but kind to you Egg. I don't see what your problem is.'

At that Egg stands up, and begins to walk away, but suddenly turns and strides up to me. 'I loved her before you even knew she existed. I've given her so much and she doesn't even notice because you're there now. Or whoever it was she gave head to last night, or whoever the fuck it is with a cock willing to give it to her. She loves you Will Hargreaves, but I don't think you really see that. You just see reasons for jealously, those things that could stand between you. Well congratulations, she's finally given you what you want. The fuck of your life.' And with that she turns on her feet and storms out of the marquee, into the black Devon night.

When Sarah returns with Marley, she is grinning, and comes rushing across the marquee and hugs me tightly, kissing me passionately on the mouth. 'You're never going to believe what's happened,' she enthuses, still cradling me in her arms.

'What?' I ask, trying to keep the anger at bay, trying not to think of what Egg said.

'I met a record producer; he said I should come to London, cut a few tracks in the studio.'

'I told you she was hot,' Marley cuts in.

'I already knew that Marley.' I spit his name. 'If you don't mind, I'd like to be alone with my girlfriend.'

'Don't worry about it man,' he taps Sarah on her shoulder, 'come see me tomorrow, I'll introduce you to some people.'

'Thanks Marley,' she says. Even though this man is helping her I can tell she is nervous in his presence, like she needs him to go so she can breathe again.

'When the talent's as good as you, any effort's worth it,' he runs his hand down her arm and squeezes her just below the elbow, 'have a good night. And remember tomorrow.'

'Goodnight Marley,' Sarah says, and as soon as he is out of the bar she spins on her heels and looks at me, 'That was rude.'

'I'm sorry; the guy gives me the creeps.'

'Make an effort for me. Please Will.'

I look at her, and feel anger draining from my body.

'Okay,' I acquiesce.

'Good. Now, let's get back to our tent, I want to feel your skin against mine.' She grabs hold of my hand and leads me out of the marquee.

In the tent Sarah nestles against me, her arm around my waist, her breasts pressed against my skin, and her lips playing with my nose.

'So what did you and Egg talk about while I was gone?'

'Not a lot. She said she wanted to get an early night.'

'That's strange; I saw her walking by the food trucks.'

'Maybe she wanted to stretch her legs before sleeping.' I rub the small of her back with my fingers, and she stirs and kisses my lips. 'I'm sorry about earlier,' I say, 'about snapping at Marley.'

'I've forgotten it already.' She kisses me again, but stops almost as quickly, 'what's wrong Will?'

'It doesn't matter.' I make out her eyes in the dark, open wide, glistening for me. 'I love you Sarah Crowe.'

'I know. And I know you. Something's wrong. What is it?'

'Egg and I had a fight.'

'About what?'

'You.'

'Me?' I can almost see the realisation cross her face. 'She told you that some prick tried it on?'

'Yeah. And you kissed him.'

'I'm sorry.'

'I don't care. You were drunk and high. We do stupid things sometimes.'

'We do. I never meant for it to happen.'

'I forgive you. Do it again I won't be.'

Sarah pulls in tighter to me and kisses my chest, resting her head just below mine. The two of us lay like that for a while, the heat of our bodies warming one another, when I feel her body start to shake, and I realise she is crying.

'What is it?' I ask her.

'I did something tonight. I didn't want too, but I was flying after the gig and I had some wine. You know how wine goes to my head.'

'What are you talking about?'

'He said it would help my contract, that's how he got me the meeting.'

'Marley? You're talking about Marley?'

I free myself from her arms, and crawl backward in the tent. Sarah tries to reach out for me, gets onto her knees and tries to come towards me. I see the tears streaking her cheeks. 'It's not my fault.'

'What did you do?'

'He asked me...' She begins to cry uncontrollably and collapses onto the sleeping bag. I look at her for a moment, unsure how to act, before crawling back over to her and place a hand on her shoulder. 'I sucked his cock.' The vulgarity of her admission shocks me.

'Why?'

'He said I would be guaranteed a contract.'

'You stupid girl.' I spit at her.

'I never meant... I thought...'

'But that's it, you didn't think. Jesus he used you and you didn't... You could have told him where to go. Fucking punched his lights out. The...' I feel my own hands clenching into fists.

'Don't.' Sarah pleads, her hands gripping me. She kisses me on the leg. 'I hate the man too, but...'

'You let him use you. You sucked another man's cock. You snog another man the night before. I don't know what to think Sarah. Hate him... I want to fucking kill him for defiling you...'

I free myself from her grip again, and pulling on my shirt and underwear, I unzip the tent door and begin to march across the campsite. I hear Sarah call after me, but ignore her pleads to come back.

The campsite is in near darkness. A few fires are burning, and a few people sit around one, some playing instruments.

'Anybody know where Marley is?' I shout at them.

'In his tent, with some lady. I wouldn't bother him.'

'Which is his tent?'

'The one nearest the stage. But I told you man, don't interrupt him.'

I ignore their warning and carry on towards the stage. I feel rage coursing through my veins. I imagine smashing Marley's head against a brick wall, about seeing his blood pour from him like a river. Then I see Sarah on her knees before him, doing that act, and I begin to run towards the tent.

'Marley, getting your fucking arse out here!' I scream, kicking the side of his tent.

'I'm busy, come back later.' He shouts from within.

'I'll give you busy.' I reach down and begin to unzip the tent door.

'What are doing man?' He shouts. Inside the tent I hear a young female voice shriek. 'I'm busy.'

I reach into the tent and see Marley naked, a young woman beside him, also nude, trying to cover herself with a sleeping bag. I grab Marley's leg and try and pull him from the tent.

'What the hell is your problem?' He shouts at me, trying to kick me away.

'You abused my girlfriend.'

'Whatever she did she did willingly.'

Again I reach into the tent and try and pull him out, when I feel a pair of arms grab me and pull me backward.

'Please don't hurt him Will,' Sarah is holding me.

'He deserves to be hurt.'

'Maybe, but not by you right now.'

'That's right sweetness, you tell him.' Marley says.

'Speak to me again and I might not hold him back.'

'Do that and I can't guarantee your contract.'

'I don't want your contract. It's worthless to me. It's only because you got me so drunk I did what I did.' Sarah pulls at me hard, trying to turn me away from Marley. 'Just leave him.'

'You slept with another girl?' The young woman next to Marley speaks.

'No. That cheap broad tried it on with me, desperate to get a record contract.'

Hearing that Sarah releases her grip on me, and I turn quickly, charge into the tent and punch Marley in the face, as hard as I can, then retreat quickly.

Just as Sarah comes storming past me and punches and kicks Marley, knocking him back to the ground.

'You lying bastard,' I hear the other woman say, and hear the unmistakable sound of a slap. 'I don't want to see you ever again.'

Sarah and I ignore the rest of the argument as we walk back across the camp, drained, ignoring the faces gathered in the shadows that had been watching my actions. Somewhere in the darkness I hear a round of applause, and someone shouts, 'He should have been punched a long time ago.'

As we walk, Sarah's hand reaches over towards mine, and for a moment our fingers touch, but I retract my hand, stop and look at her. 'I'm really sorry Sarah. I don't think I can do this either.'

'I'm sorry too.'

'I don't care about Marley. We forget that one. But you still flirted with him, still lead him on. You must have done the same last night with that other boy.'

'I don't mean too. They were stupid mistakes. I'm sorry. Don't break up with me Will. I don't think I could take it.' She reaches out to me, with both hands, her eyes pleading with me. Her lower lip quivers. 'Please. I love you too much for this to happen.'

'Sometimes it's all too much.' I look at her for a moment, wordless thoughts ricocheting in my mind. 'I'm going to sleep in the van tonight. We'll talk tomorrow.'

And then I turn my back on her and walk away. She does not follow.

4.

The Last Winter

'Good morning sleepyhead.' I feel a hand rub my head, fingers slipping through my hair, and lips touching my forehead. 'You had a good sleep. You looked beautiful sleeping; I could have watched you for hours.'

'You were watching me sleep?'

'I like to watch people sleeping, there's something really sexy about it. I used to sneak into my parents' room late at night and watch my father sleeping.'

I open my eyes and look at this woman I am laying next too, at this peculiar, alien face. She has dark black hair, tied back behind her head, and she wears too much mascara. Her brown eyes scan my face and she kisses me again quickly on the forehead.

'I like kissing you. You taste really good, like scrambled eggs and peaches.'

'Scrambled eggs *and* peaches?'

'It's what you make me think of. Scrambled eggs, peaches, and sometimes black pudding. Don't ask me to explain the black pudding, I don't think I could. What smells do I remind you of?'

'Smells? Well any natural smell is masked with that perfume you wear.'

'You don't like my perfume? What's wrong with my perfume? It costs me a small fortune to get that.'

'Hey, hey, calm down, I didn't say I didn't like the perfume.'

'Well that's good, because I can't have any boyfriend that doesn't like the perfume I wear. It just wouldn't work.'

Her using of the word *boyfriend* shocks me, and suddenly I realise where I am. That I am in her room, that I slept with her, that I had too much to drink last night, and that the hangover forming in my head like a malignant mass is going to affect me all day. All I want right now is to turn back over and sleep, and wake up in my own bed in a good few hours.

'So what are we doing today? I thought we could do something. There's a special screening of Tarkovsky's *Solaris* at the cinema. I heard that's good, we could see that. I remember you saying you liked films, so we could do that.'

The idea of seeing the film does interest me, but the more she speaks the more I realise that I don't want to do anything with her.

'What's wrong William?' She asks, seemingly reading my mind.

'Nothing,' I lie, not wanting to fight with her this morning.

'You're avoiding something. I know what it's like with you. We've been going out for three weeks four days now. I think I know when you're hiding something from me, so don't deny it.'

I didn't realise I was going out with her. 'We just happened to have slept together a few times, that doesn't mean we're going out.'

'It does. We're going out William.' I don't like her calling me William. 'Everyone knows we are. Down at the students union bar, they all said to me, 'You're lucky to be going out with

William Hargreaves. You know who he used to go out with?'
and I told them, ''yeah I know I am.' I saw you with that Sarah
bint. I don't know what you ever saw in her, she's a slapper.'

'You have no right to talk about Sarah.' I snap.

'Sorry. I'm just saying. Everyone knows we're going out.
And don't say we're not, because why would you keep coming
around to see me. You knocked on my door at ten o'clock last
night; you came up to my bedroom and did all those things to
me. I didn't ask you to. You gave me bruises, look.' She lifts
up her pyjama top and reveals a small bruise. 'And this,' she
pushes her hair back to reveal where I had been kissing her neck,
revealing a reddened mark. 'And what was with all that mistress
Liz stuff? Weird.'

'Has it really been four weeks since we started this?'

'Yeah.'

'I never thought of it as going out with each other.'

'You thought I was just sex? That you could come and have
your wicked way whenever you wanted, without any obligation?
I'm not a hooker William. We're going out. At least I hope we
are.'

'I guess we have been.'

'So what are we doing today?'

I look at her, at her thin lips, and pale face. At her small, pert
breasts, slightly revealed through her pyjama top, and at her
fingers, adorned in silver jewellery. 'You want to see that film?'

'If you want to.'

'Ok. That's what we're doing. It's Will Hargreaves and Liz
Walker on a date. We're going on a date.'

I agreed to meet Liz at the cinema later that afternoon, made
my excuses, said I had an essay to write, and left her standing in
her room, blowing me kisses. I smiled at her weakly, entertained
by her efforts, even slightly touched by them, but I just knew she
was trying too hard. That by doing so she might be pushing me
away.

Now, walking along the Cam, I tried to remember how the two of us had met. The last few weeks had been such an alcoholic blur, ever since things ended with Sarah. My mind fired for a second with the memory of driving back from Devon – the silences in the van, the jokes against me that Egg made, and then I just dropped them off outside her flat and drove off, not even saying goodbye. It was easier that way. I looked up and saw the smoke trails of aircraft, and wished for a moment to be taken off somewhere exotic, where none of this existed, where I could think without having to think. Where I could be at peace. After Sarah left I no longer felt able to stand, knocked down by the avalanche of emotion and bitter words and tears.

No, I couldn't think of her now. Liz was my girlfriend now, no matter how much she failed to register in my heart. I did find her attractive, obviously, once. I have vague memories of her at a party, where I drank too much, mixing the drinks casually, not caring what effects they might have on me later. I sat next to her on an oven, it seems bizarre in memory now, but I sat on an oven, held her hand and sang drunken songs with her. Sometime after the sun rose for the new day I remember her kissing me and that I had passionless sex in her bedroom, that she performed so many different sexual acts upon me, trying to get me to like her. I remember wishing I could be grateful.

Now I regret asking her out. I cannot believe I even contemplated dating her. I feel disgusted for kissing her, not because she had any flaw, but because I led her on, that I gave her the belief that I might be able to love her.

I come off the path beside the Cam into the centre of Cambridge, and walk along the city streets, between the ornate buildings, glancing occasionally at street names and shop names, and at the faceless people walking around me.

Then the rain started to pour and I ran down the street, quickly, and ducked into a café door, looked straight up the place, and realised I had been coming here all along.

Sarah looks at me across the crowded café. She gives a small wave, then turns away, walking into the kitchens. This is the place she works at, and I knew that. I take a seat near the back, and wait for her to re-emerge. A minute later she does.

'What are you doing here Will?'

'I needed to see you.'

'Not now. Not here.' I see emotions screech across her face. 'Please.'

'When is your break?'

'In an hour.'

I look at her, see things I never saw before, and feel my head spinning, becoming drunk. I feel the craving to touch her, to kiss her, to be with her. She looks at me for a second, two, and then spins on her heels and storms back into the kitchen. I look at a family sitting at the table opposite me, the young boy playing with an action figure, and he looks at me quizzically, head cocking to one side, and smiles greedily, his lips chocolate stained. I look at the door Sarah just exited through, then stand up and walk back into the rain, now heavy and lethargic, pounding down onto me with force and anger.

The rain hammers down, becoming more torrential, as I stand in the small alleyway beside the café where Sarah works. My mind feels pummelled into mush by the constant pressure, and my eyes heavy, tears welling with rain. I try and think through the swamp of unfocussed emotion as to why I am standing here, watching the side door to Sarah's work place, for part of me knows it is wrong to be there. I want to walk away, but my legs feel embedded to the spot, as if the constant rain as turned my feet to roots.

The side door swings open and my eyes shoot in its direction, my heart jumping upward in my chest, hoping beyond hope that it is Sarah, but it is only another employee throwing out a bag of rubbish. He gazes in my direction, the rain already dripping from his chestnut hair, as if he is afraid of me. He tosses the rubbish into the bin quickly and breaking eye contact with me darts back into the warmth of the cafe. I imagine that man talking to Sarah now, 'your psycho ex is standing in the rain out there. He's such a freak,' and I feel a sudden impulse to feel pain, to punch the wall, kick out at something, to scream at the top of my voice.

Instead I turn away from the café and walk into town, slowly towards the cinema where I am supposed to be meeting Liz later in the day.

Nobody ever told me that love was supposed to be this hard. This hard on my heart. On my mind, my lungs, my soul. That I would feel myself being wrenched apart with every step I take, with every miniscule twitch in my body. Nobody told me any of this, and I feel excluded because of it.

Liz is waiting for me outside the cinema, though I am half an hour early. She is sitting on a wet park bench, parka coat hugging her tightly, leaning forward reading a book, that as I get closer I recognise as *The Bell Jar*.

'You're here early.' I say, almost next to her now.

'I like to be early. It gives me a chance to do some reading. I always carry a book with me, read everywhere.'

'Makes sense, I suppose. But you could have waited inside, it's soaking out here.'

'But here I get to see all the people walking about.'

'But you're reading. How can you see the people?'

'You don't understand, do you Will? It's about the aesthetic of the experience.'

I try and comprehend what she is going on about when I get a sudden flash of memory, of sitting in Sarah's bedroom one night over a year ago, and the two of us were making up nonsensical words and giving them definitions.

'What did you get up to after I left? You're drenched.' Liz breaks my thought.

'You just noticed I'm drenched?'

'Don't snap at me Will, I'm trying. There are times when this isn't easy on either of us.'

'Let's not do this film. Let's just go somewhere. We need to talk.' And I spoke those clichéd lines that I had nightmares about Sarah saying to me when we first went out, knowing how much they would hurt if she spoke them to me then. Now Liz is looking at me with eyes expressing every emotion I discern as one I would suffer. 'I'm not breaking up with you.'

'Good,' she tries to hide the bubbling anger in her voice. 'Because you haven't got any reason to break up with me.'

Liz has taken me to a small café down some back alleyway; a place I did not know existed. I order two coffees and then I take the seat opposite her and look at her. At this woman with whom I am supposed to be involved, but do not know or understand.

'What do we need to talk about?' Liz cuts straight to the point, avoiding unnecessary small talk.

'I'm not quite sure at the moment; I just know we need to talk.'

'You must have some idea. You just don't demand to talk about something without having some inclination of what it is.'

I rub my eyes, trying to force the massing hangover from my body. A young waitress places the two coffees on the table in front of us and asks if we would like anything else, but Liz chases her away with a curt 'no, we'll say if we need anything else.' I find her bluntness off-putting.

'Is this about Sarah?' She asks, emphasising my feeling.

'That's the second time you've bought Sarah up today.'

'And probably about the two hundredth you've thought of her. I know you still harbour feelings for her.'

'I was with her for two and half years. It gets complicated. But it's not about her. It's about other things.'

'Like what?'

Even though I know it is other *things*, I have no idea what they are. They are just objects that swing about in the periphery of my vision, hiding in the blind spots.

'I guess I have to be frank with you.'

'It usually helps.'

'I like you.'

'Do you? Because you don't act like you do.'

'I sort of like you.'

'Sort of? What's that mean?' Liz slides back in her chair, recoiling within herself, detecting hurt on the horizon. I see her lower lip tremble; her eyes grow wider, and then shrink. I want to hold back my words, not put this woman in turmoil.

'Love is hell.' I say, searching for the right words, hating the cliché. 'Sometimes you get into situations where you know something is right, but every word you say sounds like a knife to the heart. When it really shouldn't.'

'I've been in those situations. That's why now I just say whatever it is, because there is no way to sugar coat poison.'

'That's a strange truism.'

'For a strange person. I like you an awful, awful lot William. That's why I'm willing to fight through your feelings for Sarah. They're going to fade like dying embers, and then you'll be free of her.' I look at her, feeling strange and on edge that she is saying such strangely accurate words about me. 'I know right now you don't think you'll ever be over her, but you will be. And when you are I want you to see me. Properly see me, not like you do right now. Right now I am somebody you can bear to be with when the pain is dulled by alcohol, but in the harsh light of day you always push away. I hope that soon you'll see me in daylight, and you'll be willing to give me a chance.'

I take a sip of the bitter tasting coffee, and fight with the emotions squirming in my chest. 'I went to see Sarah today.'

'What happened?'

'Nothing. We spoke briefly, then I left. It got too much to deal with.'

'I can't stop you seeing her. I have no right to ask you to stop seeing her. But I think you should. If not for me, then for yourself. It's killing you William.'

A small candle burns on the table in front of us, the flame flickering gently, and I run a finger through it.

Outside the rain is pounding the street again.

'Have you ever been in love Liz?'

'I could be. I once sat with my friends and we were all drinking red wine, talking about men, about relationships and sex, a girl's night in. Somebody asked, what if I met *the one*, but he was still in love with his ex, would I wait? And I said I never could. And I never could have done. But now I'm here with you. You're falling out of love with Sarah, slowly, but it's happening, and I'm waiting for you to do so. I don't know if you're *the one*, but I want to try and see.'

'You're a beautiful woman Liz. At the moment, as you've realised, I don't know what I want. Today I'm being a jerk. I'm badly hung-over, and ghosts are chasing around my head. I don't know how well we'll work...'

'And that's what makes it fun.'

'I guess.'

'It is. If you wanna take things slower, then I can do that. Just don't give up on me yet. I'm worth it. And you know I won't give up on you easily.' I look at her, closer this time, at her long thin fingers, at her nose, her lips, at the small earrings she wears. As I look she leans over the table and kisses me on my nose, gently, softly. 'Can we leave here? I have something I want to show you.'

Liz has taken me back to her flat. She pushes open her bedroom door, and I am surprised by the sense of ease I suddenly feel being back here so soon. She indicates for me to sit down on the bed, and takes out a photograph album from her desk drawer. She sits next to me and opens the book out between us both.

'I know what you're probably thinking. Why does she want to show me her photos?'

'I wasn't actually.'

'There is a reason,' she carries on, either missing my comment or choosing to ignore it, 'and that's because I want you to see where I've come from. I don't normally talk about it, especially not this early into a relationship, but I want you to know.'

I feel a small sense of honour at being allowed to know something secret.

'This is my sister, Lucy.'

'I didn't know you had a sister.'

'There's a lot you don't know about me, but that's why we talk, to learn about one another. Lucy has Down's syndrome.'

'I'm sorry,' I say, like it might be my fault.

'I love her to pieces. This is my mother,' she turns the page in the photograph album. 'You'll notice there is no husband in the picture. You won't find a picture of a husband in any of them. I don't know who my father is. Rather, I should say, I know who my father is, but he is nothing more than a name to me. He left when I was one.'

I squeeze her hand under the photograph album, and smile sympathetically, the gesture feeling facile.

'My mother works everyday to try and look after my sister. I send money back home too, when I can. Everybody in my family is geared to looking after Lucy.'

I glance away, a surge of bad emotion. My eyes become focused on the rain again pouring outside.

'We don't take any shit William. If somebody hurts us, we hurt them back. We protect one another. But we also have the patience of an ox. We fight for what we want. The Walker family don't give up.' Now she squeezes my hand. 'Look at me William.'

I do.

'Nothing in this life is easy. I wish it were. I care about you. I don't know if you understand that yet, or even believe that. We all have pain, and if we can share it with someone, if just for a little while, then that's time freer from the burden.'

I look at her, perhaps seeing her for the first time, 'don't say anything else Liz.'

'Why not?'

I take the photograph album from her and place it on the floor, then look back up at her, at her puzzled expression, and then I kiss her on the lips, lay her back down onto the bed and kiss her again, my hand sliding down her body to her legs, then back up again. My fingers slip inside her top. She removes it for me, then her bra, and I kiss her breasts gently, and then roll her over on the bed so she is on top of me. She pulls my jumper and t-shirt off and licks my stomach, her fingers undoing the zip on my trousers, fumbling around inside my pants, and she begins to pleasure me with her fingers and mouth.

'I've got a condom in my wallet,' I say, and in one quick move she throws me the wallet while still performing the sex act upon me.

As I remove the condom, she slides back up my body, kisses my chest, neck, cheek, mouth. 'Do you know William that this is the first time you've made love to me sober. I'd say we're moving in the right direction.'

Liz has her arm across my chest. Her eyes are closed, and she seems to be sleeping. I lie there, trying to think of different things, trying to keep my mind focussed.

I watch a fly buzzing the windowpane noisily, trying to flee into the rain drenched city.

Liz rolls gently on the bed, freeing me, and I slip out from her touch and pull my clothes on quietly, then creep out of the bedroom door and walk down the corridor towards the bathroom.

Behind another of the closed doors I hear music being played, but I do not recognise the tune. As I carry on down the corridor, becoming self conscious of stepping on a floorboard, lest it disturb another resident of the property, draw attention to me, a door opens.

A young man looks at me, 'Hi,' he says nervously, 'you must be Liz's fella.'

'I think you could describe me like that.'

'Is she in her room?'

'Sleeping.'

'And you're sneaking out?' Not very noble. Hope you left her a note.'

'Actually I was looking for the bathroom.'

'With your coat? Stop messing her about mate. She's doesn't deserve that.'

'I know. She's a lovely girl.'

This man interrupts me, 'I don't care about what or what you don't think of her. Just don't mess her about. Nobody deserves that.' He leaves me standing in the hall and disappears into the bathroom.

I stand there for a moment, unsure of the correct thing to do, for in a way, both options seem right.

Liz wakes as I push the door to her bedroom open again. She stirs in her bed, and rubs sleep from her eyes, looking at me through a haze, and then a small smile spreads across her lips.

'Have you been somewhere?'

'Too many places,' I answer cryptically. 'I'm back now.'

I sit down on the bed next to her, and play with her toes under the covers.

'Let's go out this evening,' I say to her, 'I really feel like doing something, like a proper couple. A night on the town.'

'I'd like to do that too.'

I lean forward on the bed and kiss her on the lips, and she grabs me around the waist and pulls me down, turning as I go, and the two of us stay there as the early evening traffic rushes on by outside the window.

I kiss Liz goodbye at the door, and tell her I'll be back at nine to take her for a night out, already formulating plans, and places to go, the things I am going to do. Walking down the street I cannot help but smile, not bothered what the passer-by's think of me, with this wild crazy look upon my face.

The city streets glisten after the rains, and passing under a street sign I see rivulets of water on a spider web, and stop for a moment to look at it, my emotions curiously blissful.

And then, walking down onto the pathway beside the Cam, I think of Sarah. A strong flash of her face in my subconscious and a memory of her laugh. It knocks me backward, and I realise the stupidity in thinking of her anymore, that she is a woman no longer in my life, and that I cannot spend my days living in the past.

Sitting down on a bench, looking out over the Backs, I try and banish the memories of that woman from my mind. I try and picture Liz's face, and surprisingly it comes, stronger than I ever believed it could, and I feel a weight being eased from my shoulders. A voice in my head tells me that this is all normal, that I will never be entirely over Sarah, that she was such a large part of my life, she will be forever remembered, but it is now time to move on, to accept that I have. My life is on another river now, and it is down that I now drift.

I stand, and carry on down the footpath, watching a duck swimming in the waters, and think about the evening, that moment when I will be stepping out with Liz, with the woman who is now my lover, however strange that notion may still feel to me.

When I meet Liz at the door of her flat, the days rain have ceased, at least temporarily, and there even feels as if there is a little warmth in the air. She is wearing a light blue dress, her hair is tied back in a ponytail, and she has painted her nails a light red. I kiss her gently on the lips, and then taking her hand, say, 'Let me have the pleasure of escorting you to the number seventeen bus to the city centre.'

'You couldn't book us a taxi instead?'

'Of course I could. It's parked around the corner. I wouldn't make you ride a bus in such a lovely dress. I'd have waited until I had my wicked way, then give you the bus fare home.'

'You cheeky sod,' and she slaps my arm playfully. 'Who says you're going to get your wicked way?'

'I'm an expert womaniser, didn't anybody tell you that?'

'No. But somebody should have warned me that you're an egotistical bastard!'

Liz takes my arm and the two of us walk down the short path to the road, and then carry on down towards the waiting taxi cab.

'So where are we going?'

'A bar then a club I thought. My treat.'

'Sounds good. Then back to yours for my treat to you?' Liz's voice cannot contain her excitement and she almost sounds giddy.

I open the taxi door for her and she gets in, I close the door and walk around the other side of the vehicle and climb in too.

'Didn't think there were any true gents left in the world,' the driver comments, looking at us both in the rear view mirror. 'Where to then folks? The Ritz? Raffles?'

'Town centre,' I reply, the words sounding dreadfully unromantic, and I yearn to say Paris or Casablanca instead. Not to be visiting a local bar.

'Whatever's your pleasure,' the driver says, and pulls out into the street

Liz reaches over and squeezes my hand, looking at me with bright eyes, and I rub her fingers, my mind easing into thoughts of this woman, of this avenue down which I now stroll, and wonder for a moment where it will take us, about where this will all end, and how.

***

The disco lights swirl around, casting iridescent shadows on the walls, on the faces of the hundreds dancing around us, into the eyes of my lover, now bathed in green light and seen through a deep alcoholic stupor. Liz is dancing, her hands weaving across her face, dancing excitedly in union with the music. Her eyes are closed, and though I am dancing with her, I am watching those that dance around us, at Liz's face, at the swirling, giddy lights. It all seems such a blur, such a frenetic, charged blur.

Liz's arms are then around me, 'are you sure you're alright. You don't want to go sit down somewhere?'

'I'll be fine. Just need a glass of water. I'll be back, you carry on dancing.'

Liz squeezes my arm, and then I leave the dance floor, watching for a second as she resumes dancing with one of her friends. Cutting between other revellers I make my way towards the bar, and mix into the gathered people, all waiting to be served. It takes a good ten minutes for anybody to finally serve me, and once the water is in my hand I swallow it all in one quick gulp and head back down towards the dance floor. Stopping at the railing that overlook the dance floor, I scan the people, looking at the excitement and merriment on the faces of those gyrating to the music, but fail to see I Liz's face.

Figuring that she too has the left the dance floor, I begin walking in the direction of the seats they had taken earlier, hoping to find them there when I see Sarah walking towards me.

'Hiya!' She exclaims and throws her arms around me in a tight hug. I allow the gesture for a moment and then free myself. 'I'm really glad you're here, I haven't seen you for so long, not properly.'

'You saw me earlier today,' I say, a sense of discomfort swimming in my veins.

'That wasn't properly. This is properly, where we're having fun.'

I look at her now. She is wearing a yellow t-shirt and black trousers, and I cannot help but feel a strong sense of attraction to her. Something stirs in my memory, something of long ago, of something important. How I first saw her.

'Come and have a drink with me, I wanna catch up with you.' Her words are slurred, her behaviour drunken. She slips her fingers in around mine and tries to drag me back in the direction of the bar.

'I'm here with someone tonight,' I explain to her, hoping that will ease the festering emotions.

'That floozy Liz. Yeah I heard all about you two. Egg told me she saw you in town, that you look uncomfortable with her. She said you looked like you had doubts.'

'Maybe I did when she saw me.'

'But not now?'

Her question sounds more like a statement in my mind. I am reminded of moments when Sarah seemed to be so attuned to my state of mind that it seemed as if something supernatural was occurring.

'I'm with Liz now.'

'I'm just asking for a drink, a chance to say hi. Not a shag. Come say hi to Egg, I'm sure she'd love to see you.'

'Somehow I doubt that.'

'Well maybe not Egg. But the others. I don't know what happened with us. We shouldn't have stopped being friends.'

Sarah tightens her fingers around mine and moves in closer to me. I can feel her alcoholic breath on my skin. I can see the redness of too much drink flashing through her eyes. She looks like she might be about to kiss me.

'Have you been singing lately? I haven't heard much news.'

'Occasionally. Let's not talk about my career. Let's talk about you.'

She nestles her body in closer again to me, but I do not pull back as quickly as I hoped I might. I feel attraction to her again.

'Just a chat, not too long. I've got to rejoin Liz.'

'I saw her talking with her friends; they won't miss you.'

Sarah, her hand still entwined with mine, leads me back up the small flight of stairs, and to a small booth near the back of the nightclub where I see Egg and the rest of Sarah's friends. A few of them acknowledge me, and Egg gives a very drunken wave.

'Egg's a bit too stoned tonight,' Sarah explains, 'she's been talking about the governmental conspiracy against us. We're letting her ride it out.'

Sarah indicates for me to slide into the booth, and then sits next me, trapping me between herself and Egg, and the table that is in front of us, bolted to the floor. Sarah's hand slides onto my leg, and she turns to face me properly. A voice in the back of my head keeps asking me what I am doing, sitting here with this girl.

I talk for a while about the small things – about how my academic work has been progressing, about her plans to go on holiday to Australia with Egg once their course has finished, and as the evening slides on by, the conversation drifts back to more familiar ground.

'I do miss you at times Will,' Sarah begins. 'We both made too many stupid mistakes when we were together. Got too involved too quickly.'

'Maybe.' I reply, rather apprehensively.

'You were like a married couple. Got on my fucking tits,' Egg slurs her words, and then falls back into her drugged stupor.

'Ignore her,' Sarah comments, seemingly embarrassed by her friend. 'Do you ever miss me?'

I cannot ignore the leading nature of her question. 'For a while, yeah. All the time. But it didn't work, did it? So we move on.'

Sarah leans in closer to me, her hand brushing up my trouser leg, towards my crotch. 'We don't always have to be moved on. I still think you're the sexiest man I've slept with.'

I want to laugh. 'Somehow that sounds like a compliment and insult all at once. I have a girlfriend now, I quite like her. It might work.'

'I had another boyfriend for a while too. A rugby player called Tim. He was a wanker. I miss you Will; I want to be back with you.'

I hope that her words are nothing more than drunken rambles. Taking her hand in mine I lift it up off my leg and look her straight in the eyes. 'I'm sorry Sarah. It's over now, it's got to be. I don't know how often I've wanted you to come back, say those words to me, but now I can't hear them. I'm with someone else, and I've got to go rejoin her.'

I see Sarah's eyes beginning to well up with tears, and I feel a sudden obligation to sit with her, let her cry on my shoulder. But I squeeze her shoulder quickly, and then manage to clamber out from behind the table and stand up.

'If you want to talk another night, when we're both sober, then maybe we can. But this right now, it just can't be happening.'

She looks up at me with pleading eyes, and I have to look away, as for a moment, maybe two, I want to kiss her. Want to be back with her.

'Goodnight Sarah.'

I turn and walk away from her, heading back into the throng of people. As I walk I swallow, resist the urge to turn around and look back at her. My heart pounds with the ricochet of emotional turmoil. I hate myself all at once for feeling any urge of attraction towards her, and for knowing that if I had been more inebriated, that I would have kissed her, that I would have made such a stupid mistake.

I feel an arm grab mine, and I turn around expecting to force Sarah away, but Liz stands there, looking slightly puzzled.

'What happened? You were gone ages.' She says.

'I met some old friends, just had a chat. I'm back with you now.'

Liz kisses me on the lips.

'Let's dance.' I take her hand in mine, 'I really feel like letting off steam.'

The music is fast, sometimes too fast, and I dance frantically, trying to keep rhythm with the beat. Liz tries to keep up, but failing too, just dances opposite me as best she can. I close my eyes and retreat into my mind, trying to force all the bad emotion, all the bad thought and bad memories away, to lock them tightly in my mind, cast adrift. Forgotten.

And then somebody grabs my waist and pulls me downward, lips connecting, and I respond, kissing back hard, but before the face is recognised, I know the kiss. I know I should pull away instantly, but I kiss longer, it feels right somehow, it feels natural. It feels wrong.

I push Sarah away.

'I just had to know,' Sarah shouts at me over the din.

'What the hell is going on?' Liz screams even louder. 'You're not fucking her again, I hope!' Liz slaps me and begins to storm away.

I shout her name but she does not turn back. I try and chase after her, but I lose her in the crowd. I stop, try and spot her, but Sarah is before me.

'Thank you very much,' I spit at her, 'just get lost.'

'That kiss tells me you still fancy me. You put emotion into it. You knew it was me. I love you Will, I've never stopped. I might be drunk, but I want to be with you. I love you.'

Sarah kisses me again, trying to force her tongue into my mouth, but I push her away. She slides a hand around my waist and grabs my backside, and tries to pull me close. I feel her breasts against my body. She kisses me again. The world swirls around us, the disco lights scorching my retinas. I kiss her back, but push her away almost as quickly again. I feel hard.

'Leave her. Leave here. We can leave here. Go back to mine. I'll fuck your brains out. I'll suck your cock, do anything you want. I can be Mistress Sarah, we can do anything.'

She kisses me again, harder, and I force my tongue into her mouth this time, this kiss more passionate. With her free hand she grabs my crotch and rubs. I feel harder. I close my eyes, squeeze her buttocks. And then it happens. I see Liz. In my minds eyes: I see Liz.

Breaking free of the kiss, of the contact, I hold Sarah's arms.

'Look, you can drive me wild, I know that. You know that.'

'Let's go be wild then.'

'We can't. If we do this, we'll regret it straight away. It would just be sex.'

'And what's wrong with that?' She tries to kiss me again, but I stop her.

'Things are just beginning to work with Liz now. You're a gorgeous woman Sarah, and the time we had was fantastic, but it is over. Things with Liz have a chance of being great too. I have to chase that. It's not worth losing it over a casual fuck.'

'It'd be the fuck of your life.'

'Maybe, but it's not worth it. Not now.'

Sarah shakes her head. 'I've never known one man more willing to throw such a good thing away to pursue a pipe dream. Sometimes you're a fool Will Hargreaves, a complete and utter fool. I played my cards, I lost. Good luck.' She kisses me on the cheek.

'Have a really good night Sarah. And goodbye.'

I release her arms and turn around and walk away, holding my head high. Behind me I know Sarah is contemplating pursing, but somehow I know she will not now. Somewhere else, further down the line I might have to deal with her again, but right now, in this moment, the only thing on my mind is finding Liz, fighting it out with her, reconciling this relationship before it totally explodes, and hoping, beyond all hope, that it might just work.

Are you here now? Does any of this mean anything to you yet?

As one life fades distinctly into another, the ephemera of the past sinking into the still waters of what was, there is another wave forward, into your third life, into the period of certainty. Or of what you thought was certain. You find it amazing now that life can play such tricks upon you, that fate can be such a cruel mistress.

But Laura is here, finally.

And you are still running, still hiding, still lost.

Can she pull you out? Is Laura to save you too?

PART THREE

LAURA
1997

1.

Laura. How to tell you about Laura?

Laura is my world. She is singly the most important person to have ever entered my life. The day she walked into our office she breathed in a whole new way of being, blew away all those cobwebs of the past, gave me a way to start fresh.

Only life is never that simple. It does not allow itself to be.

So Laura. How do I tell you about Laura? Is it now time?

2.

Laura. The girl with the golden hair, the deep blue eyes. The girl with the laugh that makes me smile. The girl who makes me smile and laugh. That is enough. What more do you really need?

I met Laura through work. The day she began work at our offices, she walked in and the whole of time seemed to shift, to protract. Like slow-motion in a movie. Walking her sexy, confident walk. A real independent woman. Beautiful. So beautiful. Everything seemed unreal, that a woman such as her could be coming into a place like this. Truth is, she probably just walked in and I thought: I like her. But memory never allows you to remember like that.

She was a year younger than I, had worked for six years in the BBC, but David poached her for Riverbank Films. It was good to be working with a friend. He must have hired her when I was away.

'Will, this is Laura Dawn Johnson, and today is the first day of the rest of her life. Show her the ropes, old boy.' He patted my shoulder, told her she was in good hands, and left me standing in the centre of the office, feeling vulnerable. She looked at me, and I took in her clothes. A formal suit, compared with the denim jeans and t-shirt I was wearing. She had yet to learn it was informal at Riverbank.

'Any questions about anything so far?' I asked her, trying to break the ice.

'Yeah, just one. Is he… you know...?'

'Gay? Flamboyantly so since 1985.'

'I meant... Why '85?

'Long story,' I answer and she smiled. 'Something amusing?'

'I always fall for gay guys.' And then she laughed. Sweet and intoxicating. I had never heard a laugh quite like it before.

'I'm just about to go down to the set of our latest film. They're in Brighton this afternoon. Feel like coming? See how we do things.'

'It's only my first day, I feel like I should be working.'

'You will be. Come on, nobody'll mind.'

In the car I talked too much. Laura sat quietly and listened, speaking at all the right points, letting me babble on. It seemed like that afternoon I told her everything I ever had to say.

Then she asked, 'So tell me about Mr Roper.'

'David? Ah, 1985.' I glanced at her, and her mouth was wide, smiling. 'The year before David had gone to Paris, chasing a dream. He met this guy... what was his name? Gill. Guilleme. Gill got aids, and David freaked out. He fled Paris, fled himself. He came back to Abingdon, where we lived, and tried to be outrageous, but our sleepy Oxfordshire town wasn't ready for him. So he fled again. To America. Another dream – to work in the movies. He got a job on the Paramount lot, got his first TV credits on some sitcom. He met an actor, and they shared seven months, three weeks shagging down the coast of Baja California, and then the actor hit the big time. Got a lead role in a movie. Later won an Oscar. The actor, seeing his big chance at stardom coming drops David like hot potatoes and starts dating some young starlet.'

'That's horrible.'

'It gets worse. And this goes no further, ok.' She nodded her head. 'David tried to kill himself, and while he was recovering he decided it was time to come back to Britain. So he returned, told his mother he was gay – she hadn't realised, despite the clothing and the posters of men and everything else. David's carried on ever since.'

'Jesus. Sounds like he had it rough for a while. Who was the actor?'

I laughed gently, 'that's the only secret he'll never reveal, at least, not until he's on his deathbed. All I know is that this actor is on twenty mill a film, and has dated some of the most beautiful women in Hollywood today. The way he goes on about Brad Pitt, I sometimes wonder.'

She shook her head, laughing, 'imagine if it was! So how long have you known David?'

'All my life. We met in primary school. Seems like eons ago.'

'So are you're not his boyfriend?'

'Me? No. No, not at all.'

'Good,' she smiled again, and I felt her fingers touch mine, just for a second.

The film crew were on the promenade, lining up a shot, as we arrived. The director saw us and ambled over, 'It's going great,' he said, this his first feature.

'Wonderful,' I replied, getting out of the car. 'Doug, I'd like I to meet Laura. It's her first day with Riverbank.'

They shook hands, and we began walking towards the set. 'How far along are you? David said you were shooting the finale today.'

'We are. The winds been kicking up, its ruining the continuity. Sam's hair keeps changing.'

'Changing?'

'Yeah, you know. One minute it's all laying flat, the next it looks like she's in the *Bride of Frankenstein.*'

'I'm sure you'll work your magic Doug. Laura and I will sit and watch for a bit. If you don't mind.'

'Not at all. You want a coffee or something? The catering truck is back there.'

I watched Doug return to the monsoon of people, and took a seat on a nearby bench. Laura sat with me.

'The public probably have no idea how boring making a film can be, do they?'

For a second I wonder why she is asking that question, but then I realise it is small talk. 'Probably not. So, Laura, tell me something. What made you decide on Riverbank?'

'Oh, that's cruel.' She laughed. 'Your films,' she carried on, serious now. 'Riverbank seems to be making all the best British films right now. You make Working Title seem like amateurs. No offence to WT, I have friends there. But that last film, Jesus it was good. And this one – Samantha Waterson. She's like one of the biggest actresses in Hollywood right now. I mean, for you to get her then you've got to be doing something right, right? You're like the zeitgeist of studios.'

'Thanks for the compliment.'

'I always wanted to be working with the best, and now I believe I am,' she blushed.

For a second I sit in silence, listening to the hum of activity coming from the set. Doug had shouted 'Action!' and Sam was walking towards the camera with her co-star, 'and cut!'

'There's a nice restaurant in town I know. You feel like getting some lunch?'

I knew saying it that she was going to say no. It was all just too incredible, that this woman could like me. It felt like a scene from a movie. 'I'd love too, Will' she replied, just as Doug shouted out again. Action.

Laura ordered an espresso and I said the same. She takes off her heavy red coat and slips it over the back of the chair, sits down, and looks straight at me.

'What made you want to come into this business?'

She is making small talk, looking for some avenue that will lead to a discussion we can both enjoy. These seconds of romance that everyone hates.

'David started Riverbank; it was his dream, to have his own studio. He had like twenty thou or something, enough to finance one film. You'll probably know this bit. He made *Donkey Slaves*, and that grossed what, six mil at home alone. A stroke of luck; but David's always been that way, luckier than a four leaf clover.'

'So he bought more people on board?'

'Exactly. I was working over at C4 when he offered me a position. It was less pay than I was getting, but he was offering me partnership in Riverbank, so I said why not? What was I going to lose? Two thousand may have been a lot, but it was worth it. And now I make more than I did at C4, so I don't complain.' She was forcing a smile. Change the subject Will, change the subject. 'So how long have you been into film?'

'Since forever. *The Wizard of Oz* changed my life. I saw it when I was about four, and I just remember feeling something amazing, I was really happy watching it. I can quote the whole thing now. Of course, the older I got, the more I discovered. Fellini, Hitchcock, Capra, Wilder. I get moments watching films when I feel so... insignificant. I've always wanted to make a film, direct one, you know, but when I see something – like Omar Sharif coming out of the desert in *Lawrence of Arabia*, or the assassination in *The Conformist* – it's pure genius. I know I could never do something like that.'

'How do you know until you try, though?' She looked up at me. I hadn't realised she had been watching her coffee swirl in its mug. I held her gaze for a minute. 'Seriously, though, how do you know?' She was listening to me intently. 'Have you ever held a camera, shot a piece of film? Even if it's just a bird in your garden.'

'I did some shorts at university.'

'Yeah?'

'Yeah.' Her voice was sounding fragile, unsure. 'I did a film about a woman watching a man in a bar and having a fantasy about him. It was really student filmmaking at its worse. Filmicly a rip-off from *Brief Encounter*. Sort of.'

'Hey, at least it's not another *Reservoir Dogs*.'

'They all do that now, don't they? The amount of promo reels I sat through at the Beeb – boys with guns. Every one of them a piece of shit. Lots of men pointing guns at each other and shooting, with tomato ketchup as blood.'

'But one of them might go onto make the next *Godfather*.'

'There's just so much derivative cinema. It's good to see a film company dedicated to unique visions.'

'You do know you already have the job, right?'

She laughed, took a sip of her coffee, and looked at me again. 'So what about you? What films turn you on?'

Now it is my turn to look down at my coffee, my turn to act, to play the game. Look up now, at her blue eyes, and speak.

I talk to Laura for a long time about the films that have sparked my passion. 'You really do like cinema, don't you.' She again smiles at me, and I realise how much I like this woman smiling at me. That nobody has smiled at me like this for a long time. The films I have mentioned she has liked too – a few exceptions, some she has not heard of, but I promise to lend them to her – and the conversation drifts aimlessly around the arts, like the milk swirling in my coffee cup. She listens to soul music, cannot stand hip-hop and rap. Really likes someone I've not heard of called *Harold Melvin and the Bluenotes*, and I make a mental note to buy one of their CDs when I get back to London.

'I think we should get back and check on Doug and the Bride of Frankenstein,' I say, not wanting to cut this short, but afraid of stagnation setting in.

Before I have the chance to stand up, though, Laura reaches across the table and rubs my fingers with hers. 'I hope this isn't out of line,' she says.

'Not at all.'

'I want to ask you now, before things get too hard. Would you like to go out and get a meal on Wednesday night? They've opened up a new Italian on my road, and I've been meaning to check it out.'

'Are you asking me out on a date?'

I did not expect to hear her ask this of me, though I feel relief flooding into my chest that she has.

'I think I am.' She smiles.

'You said in the car that you always fall for the gay guys. You liked David this morning.' I cannot believe I am still talking, that I have not said yes already.

She blushes. 'I thought you were David's lover. That's what I meant.'

I laugh, not mockingly. With more certainness I grip her hand, and lean across the table and place a kiss on her lips, gently. Surprised at my own forwardness. 'I would love to,' I say.

Driving back from Brighton with Laura was all at once awkward and fabulous. In just a few short days I will be sitting in a restaurant with this woman having a 'date'. How juvenile that word sounds now, I don't recall using it since my university days. I have put Classical FM on and Debussy is leaping away, interrupting my thoughts and I want to turn it off, but I don't know whether Laura is enjoying it and somehow it feels strange to ask. I know the situation is awkward, that it probably is for her too.

'You can talk to me Will.' She says, reading my mind.

'I know.'

123

'Then why don't you.'

'I sort of don't know what to say.'

'Tell me something about your first love.' She asks.

'My first love?' I haven't thought about that for a long time. I think for a moment. 'Ellie, I guess.'

'How old were you?'

'About twelve. She was a little younger. I remember her hair now, isn't that strange. It was like yours, golden. My sister, Tia, befriended her. I followed them around; there were no other boys at the holiday camp. I was going to be the typical twelve year old boy when it came to girls and push them into a rock pool or something.'

'You bully.'

'Ellie turned around and looked at me, though. That look. I never forgot it; it was the most amazing look a girl had ever given me. I didn't even know girls could give looks like that!'

'And you fell in love with her.'

'Tia dragged her away. I don't think she knew what happened, but I had to follow her.' As I talked the memory of that summer in Wales came clear in my mind, from the foggy opaque to sheer transparency. And I tell her the story, the details of it, and though it feels strange to be talking of a long ago love to a potential new love, the look on Laura's face, when I glance at her, tells me to continue, that this is connecting her to me on such a level of emotion that it would now be wrong to lie or stop or exaggerate.

'That's really sweet,' Laura says. I am surprised to hear her voice, and I realise I have been talking since the A23 into central London, and I say so, adding, 'You could have told me to shut up.'

'It was sweet, though. I enjoyed listening to you.' Now she touches my hand, as I ease the car into my parking space at Riverbank Films.

In the offices David is playing table tennis with an employee. 'Look who it is, the errant wanderers! So he's had you off gallivanting around the country, has he my dear?' David puts an arm around Laura. 'Tell me honestly, is Doug doing an absolutely smash-up job down in Brighton, or is he fucking it up Michael Winner style?'

'He seemed to be doing fine.' Laura seems uncertain as to whether she has said the right thing.

'Good, good. And how was your first day with Riverbank?'

Laura looks at me, then back at David. 'I think it was really good.'

'I think? Come on my darling, you're with Riverbank, it's gotta have been absolutely dreamlike. Talking of dreams – imagine it – Brad Pitt is interested in the Cartwright script. I've been flirting with the agent, turning on the old magic.'

David walks away and Laura looks at me, perplexed. 'He's just in hyper mood. It happens on Mondays.'

'Why Mondays?'

'Why not?'

And she laughs.

Laura wishes me goodnight in the car park, but as she walks towards her car I rush after her.

'Remember tomorrow, don't bother with the suit.'

'And I bought it special.'

'Well you can wear it if you want. We don't dictate fashion here.'

She smiles.

'I really enjoyed your company today.' Another smile. 'What I mean to say is I think you'll fit in well here.'

'Thank you. I enjoyed today too.'

The conversation is stilted. I feel like we're acting in a bad soap opera. 'I just wanted to say goodnight.' My head feels like mush.

She leans back against her car and holds the keys in her hand. 'I'll see you tomorrow.' With her free hand she touches my elbow and leaves her hand there a few seconds. 'Goodnight Will.'

I feel like a schoolboy. This is all so unbelievably stupid. She is looking at me. She is smiling at me. She turns slightly and puts the key into the lock. Then I move, neurons firing, and my mouth presses against hers and I kiss her hard. She responds, slipping a hand down my buttocks, gripping tightly. I have no memory of how long that lasts, just that it happens, and then she pulls away.

'I hope that wasn't too forward,' I apologise.

'Not at all.' She exhales loudly. 'I've not been kissed like that for a long time. It felt…' she searches for the word, 'it felt good. Unexpected, but good.'

'It was unexpected for me too. I didn't know I was going to do that.'

'I'm glad you did. Do you want to go get a drink? There's a pub I know.'

I look at my watch, and know that I have somewhere else to be soon, but the pull to go with her is strong.

'If you're busy though,' she says, 'we don't, you know…' Her voice trails away.

'I'm supposed to go see my father, he's not been well.' She looks disheartened. 'Maybe just one pint. I can't stay long.'

'Neither can I. It just seems stupid not to take this chance.'

The pub she takes me to is quiet, old-fashioned. The barman looks like he's been doing this job since the 1950s. I order a glass of white wine for Laura and a half a *Fosters* for myself. The two of us take a table near the back, away from the game of dominoes a few elderly looking gentlemen seem deeply engaged with.

'So what's wrong with your father?' Laura asks. I wonder if she feels guilty about asking that question, because she seems to blush and proffer a comforting glance.

'Pneumonia. He thought it would be a good idea to go shopping during a rainstorm without wearing his coat. Got chilled to the bone. He's getting like that at the moment, forgetful.'

'It happens to us all.' She says. 'We don't have to talk about this, if you don't want too. I shouldn't have been so personal.'

'It's fine.'

'It's just that you seem to be telling me so much, and I don't think you know anything about me.'

'All I know is that I like talking to you. It seems natural.'

'It does, you're right.' She pauses a moment. 'There's something I want to tell you now. While I can.'

'You can tell me anything.'

'I have a boyfriend. We're going through a break-up at the moment, but it's not happened yet.'

'Will it happen soon?'

'I hope so.'

'If you're that unhappy with him, just break it off yourself.'

I know I should be feeling something as she tells me this. Anger, disgust, hope, anticipation. Something, anything. She touches my hand and for a moment I don't know whether to squeeze hers back or walk away.

'I can't do that. Not yet.'

'What's stopping you?'

There is a pause. Then she says, 'Natalie.'

The rain is dancing on the windscreen of my car as I drive back through the darkened, dulled city streets. Pale amber lights pirouette across my eyes, shards of glass reflecting the abyss. Natalie. She had said the name; she had spoken that name and expected me all at once to know everything. It was a kick to the heart. 'Natalie's my daughter, Will. My boyfriend, Sean, he's not the father. Things get complicated with me. You don't want to get involved. Things are always complicated with me.' A girl at university once told me that her life was too complicated for a relationship and I had walked away from her. Only later I learnt this had not been a warning, but a request to go slow, to not be serious. That she was frightened. I look at Laura and her face is agonised, expectant.

'I think you should tell me everything,' I say to her. 'From the beginning.'

A car swerves out in front of me, and I jerk hard left on the steering wheel, narrowly missing the collision. I sound the horn, the noise coalescing with the cacophony of the city at night, the city falling to sleep around me. I want to sleep, but I have to get home first, through this long, encroaching night.

At home, I prepare a light supper of cheese and biscuits and retire to the living room. I spend ten minutes looking through my video collection, looking for something undemanding to watch, settling for *A River Runs Through It*, but as the opening music begins to chime, I feel the need to sit in silence and so turn the television off. I wonder for a moment about calling David, just talk to him about something banal, but I know he'll be curled up with his partner, probably having wonderful sex, and I know he would only ask about Laura. I know instinctively I cannot call her. I left the pub very quickly after she explained the situation to me, and now I wouldn't blame her for not talking to me ever again.

A child with one man, and in a relationship with another. I cannot understand how that can be, but as the scotch I've poured myself mingles with the alcohol from earlier in the day I feel the pull of sleep, the nauseous sway of the amber liquid cutting deep. I put the glass down on the table and throw my feet up onto the couch and lay down. Laura. I see her in my mind's eye. She looks beautiful, she looks like she could be in one of the movies I produce, and I think for a second about using my influence to get her onto the screen, into a movie, but I hear David's chastising voice, and brush the idea from my subconscious.

Very soon afterward, I fall asleep.

3.

'Who wants brussel sprouts?' Mum enters through the kitchen door carrying a steaming hot tray of vegetables. 'Geoffrey?'

'Let the kids have pick first. I'll have what's left.'

Once a month we try and meet like this, the whole family. Mum instigated it after she – I now realise – saw the family almost fall apart when we were children. When I was still a teenager, and wanted to be out with David and my other friends, I threw a tantrum, like some insolent child, about the necessity of gathering once a month with my family for a meal. 'It is important William,' Mum chastised me. 'It keeps up close. Keeps us strong.'

I doubted her, of course, and as I went off to university I missed these monthly rituals. I remember Sarah refusing to come to one, years ago, when she lived with me in the caravan. These moments, though, they became important. Even when I moved to London, and a few years later when Tia followed me, we still made the trek back just for this. I think because it was prescribed that we could talk at these meals about anything, that everybody came relaxed and more willing to talk than at other times.

I took the bowl of sprouts from Mum and put four on my plate, then passed the bowl onto Tia.

'It looks lovely again Mum,' Tia said, piling the food onto her plate. 'Once again you've excelled yourself.

'Wait until you taste the apple pie. It's the best ever I swear.'

Dad leaned up and kissed Mum on the cheek. 'You're always the best ever dear.'

'You have to show me more love than that to get a bigger slice Geoffrey Hargreaves.'

'Darn and blast it,' Dad laughed. 'I'll get around you one day Eileen.'

Mum sits beside him and squeezes his hand. 'You've been trying for thirty five years and haven't succeeded yet.' In the way these dinner conversations can migrate between subjects without provocation, Mum turned to Tia. 'So when's Brian coming to visit again?'

I look at my sister, 'you bought him to meet the parents. So this is getting serious.'

Brian's a fellow teacher at the comprehensive Tia works at. The sports teacher. After they met Tia confided in me one night, after a few glasses of wine, that when she was a schoolgirl, 'I always fancied our gym teacher.'

'Muscles Motton?'

'Yeah.' Tia blushed, 'I know. I saw him the yearbook photograph not too long ago, God knows what I was thinking. But the idea of a gym teacher still turns me on. Hence Brian.'

'So you're just dating him because he teaches gym?'

'And he is fit.'

'So not like Muscles Motton.'

'Definitely not like Muscles Motton.'

I have always been glad that I got on with my sister. I've had friends who haven't got on well with their family – Sarah was one – and I always thought it sad that life for them was that way. Because of the way we were I could tell Tia things before anybody else. But she had not said anything about her relationship with Brian deepening.

'We've entered another level,' Tia thought about it. 'It certainly seems more than just a fling.'

'It was just a fling?' Mum looks at her daughter incredulously.

'Staff room romance. You know how these things go. But it just seems to be working. At least I'm in a relationship. Shouldn't you be badgering Will? Sorry Will.'

'That's it. Pick on the single guy.'

'So there still isn't anyone? Nobody at all?' Dad asks. He's as much complicit in these light-hearted interrogations as Mum and Tia.

'Actually...'

They let out comic sounds of interest, Tia's face rippling with giddy excitement. 'Tell us more dear brother.'

I close my eyes, picture Laura. I can smell her. I can feel the touch of her on my body. She is that ingrained upon me already. I look at my family.

'I don't know. She might be the one.'

Tia, who was about to put a roast potato chunk in her mouth stops, looks straight at me. 'Is that serious?'

'I've not liked anybody this much since university.'

'What's the problem?' Mum asks, always the insightful one.

'She's not single. And she has a kid.'

My family go quiet for a moment.

Dad speaks first, 'Well the second point isn't a problem. But Will, if this woman is happy...'

'That's it, she's not.'

'She told you that?'

'They're breaking up. They may even be broken up now. It's why I keep checking my phone.'

'Be careful son,' Mum says.

'What's her name?' Tia asks.

'Laura. Laura Dawn Johnson.'

'Pretty name,' Mum says.

Nobody is eating. The food is steaming hot on our plates and everybody is looking at me.

'And her child' Mum asks.

'Natalie Michelle Johnson. She's one. Look guys, I know you want to know everything, but can we not? I mean, everything's so uncertain right now. I don't even know if we'll get together.'

There is another moment's silence. Dad breaks it, 'You remember Freddie? He got four numbers on the lottery yesterday.'

And with that my family moved on, to a new subject, leaving me alone. I couldn't concentrate though. Every few minutes I glanced at my mobile phone, waiting for her call, waiting for a message to say she was free, that we would soon be together.

We stayed and watched some game show; Tia curled up on the sofa, head resting against Dad, still his little girl. Mum bought out a small bowl filled with chocolate fingers, and we sat for a while, munching them, watching television, and for an hour or two I felt about ten years old again. It felt good, retreating from the world like that.

I drove Tia back to the city. Though the radio was on, playing quietly, we talked. I knew we would talk.

'So Laura...'

'So Brian...'

'Don't play games with me Will. You know you never win.'

The motorway curled out in front of us, dark and empty of traffic.

'Do you think Mum and Dad are happy?'

'Don't change the subject Will.'

'But do you?'

'Of course they are. They love each other.'

'Is that enough?'

'You don't think love can bring happiness?'

'I look at Laura. I mean, she's in this relationship, and I didn't say this at home, but he's not the father. I mean, I think she's wonderful, you know, but I've got rose-tinted specs on right now. But do the maths. That's two men in two years she's got through.'

'If you think like that Will you'll never survive in a relationship with her. You have to forget all that. It's her past, it's not relevant. If you really want to be with this woman just be yourself with her, and let her be herself. Don't go judging her before you even know her.'

'I'm not judging her. I'm just wondering... I mean she must have loved those men. So love is transitory, a fleeting thing.'

'Until you find the right one. Like Mum did with Dad. Then it can last. Look at what they've got through. They used to fight all the time when we were kids. Now they're like a pair of love sick teenagers again.'

I pulled the car over into the slow lane. 'Have you found the right one in Brian?'

Tia smiled. 'I think I might have done.'

We did not talk about our relationships again as the traffic built up as the M40 piled into the M25 and West London loomed large on the horizon, lights sparkling in the distance, humming below a vast neon sky.

4.

Laura and I spent almost two weeks in a semi-awkward relationship. It had always been one of my rules – these limitations we put upon ourselves to make life easier – do not date work colleagues. That one had come about because once, on the first week of a job, I slept with a colleague, and the next month was unbearable, awkward silence in the office, gossip behind our backs, bitching about one another. It had not gone well. The odd thing, I noticed, though, was that with Laura – yes it was awkward, yes there was that same silence in the office, but we could talk to one another, still do our job, and still, at lunchtime, sneak out back for a quick, intimate chat and a kiss. It felt illicit, like we were school kids bunking off, those cheeky kisses. She was still with the boyfriend.

'I can't break up with him, not yet.' She excused herself. 'His mother is ill. I mean really ill.'

I knew she was saying she would break up with him when his mother was well again. 'But what if she dies?'

'Will don't say that.'

'But if she does? Will you stay with him through the funeral, through everything? How long do you wait until he's ready?'

I wondered if she was making excuses, if she somehow found leading the two of us on a turn-on. Was this what did it for her? But not once did I think about ending it. I liked Laura, despite it all, I liked her, I mean really liked her. David even told me, 'the two of you, you're good together.'

The night after I dropped Tia off at her home, I lay in my bed thinking it over. What ultimatum would I give her? How long was I prepared to wait? The more I thought about it the more I realised I was willing to wait both a very long time and no more time at all. It became an agonising decision, the decision to tell her now or never. I couldn't sleep. I got up and paced. Got back into bed. It was three am.

And then she called.

'I hope this isn't too late.'

'Not all. No way. I'm really glad to hear your voice.'

'Jason and I have had that fight. He cried a bit, told me I was heartless. I'm not heartless, am I Will?'

'I don't think so.'

I hear her breathe a sigh of relief. Then, in a sexy voice, she says, 'So I just wanted to say I'm yours. If you still want me.'

I think I screamed. I think I laughed. And cried. I think I went through every good emotion. I think I woke up the neighbours.

I asked, 'can I be impetuous?'

As I drove to her flat I thought whether it was right to go straight to see her, straight after a break-up with a man whom she thought she might have loved. I needn't have worried. She was on the steps outside her flat, a cardigan pulled tight around her, her hair fluttering in the night breeze. I got out of the car and looked up at her, looked at her looking back down at me.

'I would have bought flowers but it's three am. Nowhere's open.'

'You bought yourself,' she kissed me, 'that's enough.'

On the way through her small flat, we stopped and looked in on Natalie, asleep in her crib. I looked at daughter and then at mother and a strange feeling came over me. I wanted this family to be my family. I was prepared to sacrifice anything to be here, with her, forever.

I took Laura's hand, kissed her, and we spun around into her living room. The radio was on quietly in one corner, playing something smooth and jazzy.

'I don't think I've ever done this before,' Laura said as we slid down onto her couch.

'I think the baby in the other room might refute you on that,' I smiled, nibbling her ear.

'Not that,' she slapped my arm gently. 'I mean broken up with one man and leapt into bed with another an hour later. This doesn't make me cheap, does it?'

I stopped kissing her cheek. 'If you don't want to tonight, I'll understand.'

'I've been waiting for this for weeks with you.'

'You're not cheap Laura. You're beautiful. I don't care about what you've done or not done before. I'm just interested in us and all we can be.'

Laura smiled, 'that's sweet Will.'

We kissed and made love, and the next morning found ourselves an hour late getting into the office. As we walked in together I caught David in the corner of my eye, giving me the thumbs up. Everybody could tell. Everyone knew. Laura and I were now dating.

5.

A Year Later

Natalie was screaming. In the bed beside me, Laura shifted, stirred.

'It's OK honey,' I say, kissing her on the cheek. 'I'll see to her.'

'What would I do without you?' She answers tiredly, dreamily.

Pulling on a t-shirt, I rub the exhaustion from my eyes and glance at the alarm clock, it reads 04:36. *Does she ever sleep?* I think, shaking my head to try and wake and walk into the adjacent room.

'What is it this morning, Princess? New diaper? Bottle?' I look at Natalie in her crib, at her agonised face, and lift her up, see the small pool of urine. 'Diaper. It's always diapers with me. I bet you do it on purpose, don't you?' Natalie stops crying, a strange look of bemusement on her young face. 'I've been living with you for six weeks now and I think I've seen enough of your wee to fill a small valley, yes I have.' I sometimes try and make child-talk with Natalie, like Laura does, but I find it foolish, so instead I talk to Natalie as if she were fully grown.

Changing her diaper, I try and think through the fog of tiredness about what I have to do today. David wants me at that meeting, saying he has something important to discuss, but he says that about every meeting, and at the moment I don't have the energy to travel to the office. Laura is going in anyway; she can make notes. Money for the babysitter, too, I must sort that out. And Laura needs more space for her clothing. And... I know there is something else, but it will not reveal itself. The quagmire has stolen intelligence from me this morning.

Bed and baby fully changed, I put Natalie back in her crib, and she falls to sleep relatively quickly. Walking back to the bedroom I see Laura is asleep again, and I stand in the shadow of the doorway watching her sleeping for a while, admiring the beauty of her face, the contours of her shoulders and her body, which I imagine under the covers. I am surprised, even now, that I had the courage to ask her to move in so quickly.

That first night, in bed with her in my home, she looked at me with soulful eyes, her hands around my waist, and she told me about how this had all begun. She was at the BBC, went out with some of the girls from work for a night on the town, and it was in some cheap club she met some cheap man, and they went back to his. Nine months later she had Natalie, and knew not who he was. She looked for that cheap man for weeks afterward but she never saw him in any club – he was just Colin, from the City. Laura had let out a fake laugh, he was probably married with kids, from Dagenham, mortgage, drives a Volvo. I laughed gently, falsely too, so she felt comfortable. 'I really like you Will, I want this to work. I want it to work like nothing else has. I've messed up so much lately. Sean, he was a huge mistake. Dagenham man, mistake. I... I want us to work out so much.' I told her it would, that I liked her too, that I could feel myself

140

falling in love. I wondered whether it was too soon to say that, but she said, 'I think I'm falling in love with you too,' and she kissed me long and hard. When she broke away, I added one more thing, to reassure her as much as I could, 'and I love Natalie. I've never met such a bright child before.' And then I saw it on her face – that look of love, that music spreading there.

And now she is asleep in my bed, and Natalie in the next room. I decide to leave them sleeping and walk down to the kitchen in my underwear and t-shirt. I turn on the cappuccino machine that Laura brought with her, and walk into the front room, and turn on the television. The BBC's twenty four hour news service is playing away and I press mute, just let the glow of the screen fill the room, I have no real need to watch. It's just security.

As I sit there, I close my eyes and listen to the quiet creaks and moans of my home. I realise I am in love with Laura, that this love is genuine, that I would be hurt if she left.

As I slide along towards a dreamscape, I hear the ring of the telephone bringing me back. I exhale loudly, who would be calling me this early in the morning.

'Will Hargreaves,' I say my name.

'Will, it's your mother.'

A blast of instant fear. 'What's wrong Mum?'

'I didn't know who to call.'

'What is it? Has something happened to Dad?'

'He's fine. Snoring away,' I realise I can hear him in the background.

'So what is it?'

'I was in the bathroom just now. I discovered a lump.'

'What do you mean?'

'I have a large lump in my breast. I'm scared William. I have a lump.'

Once, on some almost forgotten family holiday, shrouded in the mysteries of time, I walked along a forest path, clambering

141

over a fallen tree trunk and Mum fell and sprained her ankle. I saw her wince in pain. I recall that moment with agonising detail, even though the time and place and my age of this moment is sunken in the abyss. I watched Tia scrambling on ahead, laughing at the wings of a butterfly tiptoeing on air, and Mum held my shoulder, 'don't tell Tia I've hurt myself. The worry will only harm her.' I puzzled about what she meant, about the purpose of her warning, and how Tia could be hurt by such things.

The pattern on the wallpaper was absorbing me, taking me away from this telephone call, from this horror I am witnessing but cannot see. My mother coughing on the other end of the phone disturbs me into reality. 'I don't know what to say Mum. Do you want me to tell Tia?' And that is when your mother's warning, back in that forgotten wood on that forgotten tear of time becomes clear.

'I don't know. Maybe not yet, maybe it'll be nothing. It's just a lump at the moment. It might just be a cyst.'

'It might be. You should go see the Doctor in the morning. Is Doc Grahams still practising, he was always good.'

'He retired honey. Sent us a card, with pictures of ducks on. It was sweet. It's all full of youngsters there now; I don't think they know the difference between an arm and a leg sometimes.' I know she is rambling, but I do not have the heart to stop her.

As she speaks I look around the living room of my home, at the detritus of life catalogued on the mantelpiece, on the coffee table, at the dirty ring of age circling out on the walnut cabinet, one of Natalie's toys lopsided on the floor, Barbie arms flaying out to space, in an invisible hug.

'Mum, do you want me to come up?' I break in.

'No, don't worry about it. I can take care of myself.'

I can see Dad in the house now, sitting in front of the television, watching some quiz show, silently answering all of the questions, letting his wife scurry around taking care of everything. He would be of no use to her if things were bad, he would just collapse into the chair and expect all the ills to vanish like smoke trails rising into the sky, that this lump would just shrink, and that it would all become fine. That by answering more quiz questions life could be normal once again.

'How's Laura? And Natalie?' Mum surprises me with a tack in the wind.

'They're fine.'

'When are you going to surprise me with news of a blood grandchild?'

'What?' Her words are making no sense.

'When are you and Laura going to have a child together?'

'I don't know.'

'Have you talked about it?'

'Once or twice. Natalie's enough for now. We both have careers to juggle. It's complicated.' I hear Mum about to say something. 'Look Mum, I don't think now is the time to talk about these things, do you?'

There is silence at the other end of the line.

'Good. Now, the surgery must be opening soon, so I want you to get down there and get this… this lump examined.'

'Shall I wake your father?'

'He has to drive you there, so I think you should. And tell him. Because I know you won't otherwise. You always shield us, don't do that this time.' I have never spoken to her like this before and I shock myself.

'OK,' she says, 'thank you honey.'

'Call me later. I'll be at the office when you get out.'

She thanks me again, and as she goes to hang up I say, 'I love you,' but I don't know whether she hears my voice lost in the static.

'So darlings, have you got everything sorted out for tonight?' David asks as Laura and I enter Riverbank's main office.

'We've the sitter for Natalie. I've got to pick up my suit from the drycleaners. Other than that we're all ready to rock 'n' roll.'

'Are you excited? Your first movie premiere. With hundreds of beaming well pressed and dressed special guests. We've got Donna Air, and Richard Blackwood. Imagine Richard Blackwood in a tux, I'll get all moist at the thought.' He shook his body a little, gaining laughs from those around, though I do not laugh. Somehow David's mannerisms seem petty today.

'So long as we get front row seats we'll be happy,' Laura slides an arm around me, 'won't we honey.' When I don't respond Laura looks at me, 'I said won't we honey.'

'Won't we what?'

'Be happy with front row seats.'

'Oh yeah, sure. Yeah, you better have splashed out on us David; otherwise I'll quit and go work for Film Four!' My attempt at a joke seems forced.

'Go work for them. You'll get paid less, not have your own office, have to wear a suit and tie, not get invited to the premieres. And most importantly, you won't be working for such a handsome man.'

'And you won't be making such first class films,' another voice sounds behind us.

'Douglas Eidson! What's such a talented man doing in our offices?' David greets the director of the premiere we're watching tonight with a kiss on both cheeks. I hadn't realised Douglas was gay until that moment.

'I've come to bring champagne.' Douglas pronounces it *cham-pag-nuh*. He reveals a bottle that he had been hiding behind his back.

'My favourite.' David jumps around on the spot like a little girl, and then takes the bottle from Douglas. 'Come here you great big lummox.' He pulls Douglas close and kisses him on the lips, quickly. I detect something more there, though, like this might have happened between the two of them before. 'Let's go into the hive,' and David opens the door into the main work area of Riverbank, where the fifteen employees are busy working.

'Can I have your attention?' David booms. Some people carry on working. 'Ladies and gents I've got a fandabulous announcement so will everyone stop making us look efficient and listen to the gay guy who's about to throw a party!' The room stops and looks up at David. 'Great. As you know, tonight is the premiere of Douglas Eidson's brand spanking Riverbank produced new film, *Moonbeams Kiss the Sea*, and so to celebrate our good fortune in having this film as one of ours, I'm cordially inviting you to a booze ridden party. Debauch yourselves my good people.' He then cracks open the bottle of champagne, bubbles of white shooting out into the room, and a cheer raised, David holding Douglas' arm high into the air, and Laura looking at me, smiling wanly, knowingly.

Some of the staff have returned to work when Laura slings her arm around me.

'This is a really special day. I feel like I've achieved something with you and with this company. Doug's new film seems like a baby I've helped raise.'

I am not really sure what she is talking about, though her words do seem to make sense. 'There's something I want to tell you.'

'What?'

But David interrupts me. 'There's a telephone call for you. It's your mother. She said the gardenias are blooming, apparently they look lovely.'

'I'll take it in your office, if you don't mind?'

'I've always said you can enter my office anytime you like.' He giggles, drunkenly.

'And I've told you David, you can't have him anymore, he's mine.' Laura quickly kisses me on the cheek and I walk up towards David's office, a sense of dread rising in my gut.

'Hello Mum.'

'I went to the doctors. Took me ages to get there, the bus seemed to stop every two minutes.'

'I thought you were going to ask Dad to drive you in.'

'I didn't have the heart to wake him.'

'Well you *went* to the doctors, I suppose that's something. What did they say?'

'They're making me an appointment at the hospital. Should be soon. Do you think Laura would mind if Natalie came to spend a weekend with us?'

'What? I don't know. I never... why do you want Natalie to come spend a weekend with you?'

'I feel a need to look after a child for a while. I can't explain it. Just ask her son, please.'

'OK, I'll ask. Now, are you going to tell Dad about the lump?'

'I will do, just let me do it in my own time. I must go Will, the soups bubbling over on the stove.'

She hangs up the phone before I get a chance to say goodbye. I sit in David's office for a moment in silence, looking at the photograph on his desk of his beloved dog, and at the small pile of papers in his in-tray. Then I pick up the phone and dial the number for my sister. There are two short rings.

'Tia, its Will.'

'And how's my older brother?'

'What are you doing today?'

'Laundry. Brian ruined his football kit soccer yesterday, been cleaning up after him. Why?'

'I need to talk to you. Can we meet for lunch?'

Tia has cut her hair. Last time I saw her she was wearing it long again, just above her waist, and now it's in a Louise Brooks bob, and she seems different for it. She waves at me, and a for a second I see her as my little sister, five years old, making a mess with vanilla ice cream, but then I see the confident, working woman she is. She is wearing jeans and t-shirt today, beside her a gym bag. She is drinking orange juice.

'How are you Will?'

'I'm well. You?'

'Brian's talking about moving in with me.'

'That sounds good.'

'It is. Mum likes the idea too. She can't wait for one of us to have children. I think the idea of being a grandmother is like a narcotic for her!' I laugh, can't help but agreeing with her. 'So what's up, you sounded worried on the phone.'

Tia – always leaping into things head first. 'What's not? Everything seems to be snowballing at the moment. David's being particularly outlandish – I think he's in love again.' Why am I not telling her? Can I not face up to this problem either?

'Who's the unlucky guy this time?'

'A film director. A client. It's his business, and there's no stopping him.'

'Isn't he with someone?'

'The day I understand David's love life is the day the world ends.'

A waitress interrupts us and I order a coffee, black. I notice Tia's earrings, reflecting sunlight into my eyes, and for a second I recall something from a long time ago. 'Are you going to move in with Brian?'

'I don't know. I like my space'

I smile gently, and look at my sister. 'Don't be forced into anything, and don't let circumstances dictate anything. Make your own mind up, but be prepared to accept certain things.'

'You sound like you're talking from experience.'

And then I say it. 'Mum's not well. She's found a lump.' The light reflecting from Tia's earrings blinds me for a second, and I look down into the swirling black coffee in front of me, and Tia puts a hand to her mouth covering a silent word.

'What do you mean, 'she found a lump'? When? When did this happen?' Tia finally speaks, still cradling her orange juice as if it were a talisman that could warn away this bad news.

'She phoned me this morning. Just before I went to the office. She's been to the doctors; they're sending her for tests at the hospital soon.'

'I'll go and see her tonight, Brian won't mind. Has she told Dad yet?'

'I think so. I hope so. I told her too, but you know what she's like.'

'Oh God.' I hear fear and panic in her voice, can see her eyes dilating.

'She said herself it could just be a cyst.' I try and reassure Tia, Mum's warnings still reverberating around my head. 'I just hope she carries on like normal, until we know for sure. Remember when Dad had that trouble with his lungs, she collapsed for a week, wouldn't move. She's never taken illness well.'

'I remember one time; it was when we were in Spain.'

'And I broke my leg.'

'Yeah. She hyperventilated, Dad had to call the Doctor back out.'

'I always wondered why he came back.'

'She told me not to tell you she wasn't well.'

As I laugh at these absurdities, Tia looks at me quizzically and then begins to laugh with me, and the two of us laugh louder, more to relieve the tension than in humour.

Between laughs I say, 'I always wondered why she got so stressed about illness, and not about things that mattered, like Dad's indiscretions.'

'What do you mean? Dad's indiscretions?'

'They never told you?'

'Told me what Will?' She looks at me sternly.

'It's nothing.'

'Did Dad... did Dad have an affair?'

'Forget I mentioned anything Tia. It's all ancient history.'

'Oh my God. When? When did this happen?'

She looks at me, accusatory, then pleadingly. I look away from her, to the swirl of colours in the carpet design, then back at her. I feel heat running down my neck, and rub the palm of my hand over my left eye, forcing memory away. 'This goes no further,' I say to her, and begin to tell what I know, my words forming before her like crystalline daggers.

Laura is sitting with David and Doug, her legs up on a chair, still drinking the complementary wine. She waves giddily as I enter the offices.

'Doug's just been telling me that there's a surprise in the film for us,' she says, 'but he won't spoil it, so don't even try to find out.' She laughs. 'He's told David, though, because he's mean like that.'

I feel like walking back out of the offices, back into the cold rain, into those grey city streets. I close my eyes a moment and try and think of anything that can take me away from these people, if only for a few moments.

'Is something wrong, my boy?' I sense David moving closer. 'You look like you're about to wretch. Because if you are, I warn you, in the toilets please, we just had this carpet shampooed.'

David's voice grates. His intonation reminding me of fingers running down a blackboard. I feel like screaming out loud.

'What is wrong honey?' Laura approaches, puts one hand against my arm. 'Come on, sit down.'

I allow myself to be taken to a seat. David indicates for Doug to go fetch a glass of water, as Laura kneels down beside me. I look at her, at this woman, my partner, my girlfriend. She looks strangely unfamiliar to me in this light, then suddenly I feel as if I am sinking down under water, that the waves are now lapping over my head, somewhere, and I'm drowning, going down deeper, into the darkness.

A couple of Riverbank's employees are now gathered around, looking at me in this state, half concerned, half entranced in morbid curiosity. 'Should we call a doctor?' Somebody asks, 'he's looking white.'

'I don't need a doctor,' I snap back, instantly. 'Just give me some room.'

David begins to push people backward, ushering them back to their desks. Doug stands where he is, looking at me, and I sense he is unsure how to act. Laura begins to rub my hand, 'are you sure you don't need a doctor? You really don't look well.'

I push her hand away, and try to stand. As I push myself up out of the chair, my legs buckle, and the world spins into shadows.

My head feels sore. I can feel a dull throbbing in my skull. Every colour forcing its way into my retinas feels harsh, brutal.

'Here, drink this.' I recognise Laura's voice.

I feel my hands take a cold glass of something from her, though my eyes do not recognise any action I take. I sip the liquid quickly, and it burns as it rushes down my throat.

'Drink it slowly,' Laura says, as an afterthought.

'What happened?' I ask.

'You passed out. You're in David's office. We called a doctor, he hasn't arrived yet.'

'I'm sorry,' I say, though I am not sure why.

'Don't worry about it. You're okay now.' She cradles my face in her hands, and kisses me tenderly on the forehead, but I pull back, away from her affection. 'What's wrong?'

I feel a laugh forming in my chest, but I repress it. I want to scream out, *everything, everything's wrong!* but I do not. 'There's a lot I need to say Laura, I just don't know how to say any of it.'

'Just try.'

I swallow some more water, letting it soothe the dryness in my throat. 'I have no idea what to say first.'

Laura grabs a chair and pulls it over, then sits down opposite me, holding my hands in hers. 'Take your time.'

'I need to be on my own.'

'What's that mean?'

'I'm really very sorry. I need you and Natalie to move out. I need to be on my own.'

'You're breaking up with me?'

'No. I just need space right now. Go and stay with your mother or something.'

'Where's this coming from? I don't understand.'

'I'm sorry Laura.' I close my eyes and stand up.

'Will?'

'I'm sorry.'

I walk out of the office, Laura's tears breaking out behind me. A second later I hear the office door open again, 'Wait Will. Talk to me! Please!' But I hear no more as I enter the lift, and the metal doors clang shut behind me.

Pushing open the door to The Willows, the sound of the burglar alarm slices into my head, and I rush to silence it. Switching on the hallway light I see the message button flashing on the answer phone, and I press it without thinking.

'Hi Will, it's your father. I think something might be wrong with your mother. She has that strange look of hers that she gets when she's trying to hide something from me. I don't know what it is, but I think it might be serious. Can you call me please?' I shake my head, my mother still being as obstinate as ever, despite the cause for concern. I delete his message.

'Will please.' I recognise Laura's voice instantly. 'I don't know what's wrong, but talk to me. David and I had a talk earlier about it; we both could tell something was wrong. I called the babysitter, she's bought Natalie over to me, and we're staying with David tonight. Come over, talk to me. If I've done something wrong, I'll try and sort it out. If it's something else, I'm sure we can work it through. I love you Will.'

I exhale loudly, collapse back against the wall, and begin to cry.

And then the phone rings again, once, twice, and wiping the tears from my eyes I pick up the handset.

'Will Hargreaves,' I say it without even thinking.

'Will, it's your father.'

'Dad,' I breathe his name, my mind a swamp.

'It's your mother Will. She's just collapsed; I think you should come quickly.'

The lights are on in the front room of my parents' home. Outside the flashing blue lights of an ambulance rebound off every window, throwing the street into a strange glow. Dad stands in the doorway of his home, bracing himself against the doorframe while a paramedic stands beside him. I leap out of my vehicle, forgetting to stop the engine, and run up the garden path.

'How is she?' I shout, before I even stop running.

Dad looks at me, his eyes distilling tears.

'Are you the son?' The paramedic asks, stepping in for my father. I nod. 'Your mother collapsed. At the moment we're not sure what's caused it, but we're taking her to the hospital for a check-up.'

'She went to the doctors this morning.'

'She did?' Dad asks, his voice frail.

'She found a lump in her breast last night. She thinks it might be cancer.'

'Oh God,' my father shudders.

Inside the house I see the second paramedic pushing Mum in a wheel chair. She is conscious, I see a small bruise on her forehead, and she looks pale.

'Are you alright Eileen?' Dad's tremulous voice cuts through the night air, sounding like shattered glass.

'I'll be fine,' she wheezes, still trying to be brave.

'Will you be coming in the ambulance Mr Hargreaves?' The paramedic asks my father. He does not answer, but follows his wife down the path.

'I'll follow in my car,' I speak. 'Did you call Tia Dad?'
'No. Mum said not to worry her.'
'I'll call her. She needs to know.'
I rush back down to the car and find Tia's name on my mobile phone, pull the car door closed, and begin to follow the ambulance down suburban streets, shadows looming at me largely, as the phone in Tia's home begins to ring.

Tia meets us at the hospital. Her eyes are teary, though she has yet to see Mum. I hug her quickly.
'How is she?'
'The doctors are looking her over.'
Tia sits down, her legs tremble. 'What happened?'
'I don't know. I don't think it's anything to do with the lump she found. But I don't know. They're looking into that now.'
'Where's Dad?'
'He went in with her, wouldn't leave her.'
Coming down the corridor I see a middle aged Asian doctor. His hands are inside his trouser pockets, and he has that weathered, unemotional look that doctors adopt.
'Are you Will Hargreaves?' He asks me, and I nod. 'I'm Doctor Rajiv Patel, can we sit down?'

PART FOUR

THE LIFE BEYOND
1997

1.

The rains were clearing as I walked up the stone path towards the church. Tia's arm was around mine, her head lowered under a veil, a white tissue in her hand, which she used occasionally to dab her eyes. My freshly starched suit itched at the small of my back. In front of me Dad walked with Miriam, my mothers' sister, also supporting each other. A shard of sunlight cut across the top of the church, the puddles around our feet glistening.

'At least it's stopped raining,' I say to Tia, just to hear a sound.

She glances up at me, and I squeeze her arm. She tries to smile, but her expression cannot conceal the grief.

When I was a young child, I imagined this very day. It was while I was walking through the supermarket with Mum, and ran off down one aisle to look at toys. Mum shouted something at me, but I failed to hear her words, instead enraptured with the toy fire engine I cradled in my hands. Then I looked around to ask if I could buy it and she had disappeared. I ran back down the aisle and she was nowhere to be seen. I began walking down the other aisles, my speed increasing, heart racing, but I could not see her among the swell of people. People that now seemed huge, looming like giants, waiting to crack my bones. Running to the front of the shop, I hid behind a display cabinet, peering out occasionally, and trying to suppress my tears. And as I stood there, in the shadows, I thought what if she never returns? What if she is dead? And I imagined walking up the church pathway, her body in a coffin, and I would be carrying it on my back. Tears welling in my eyes, Mum grabbed my shoulder, 'what are you doing hiding there William?' and she pulled me out, and the thoughts slid back into my subconscious, but the swamp still festered on unseen.

'Will there be enough room for us to sit on the same row as Dad?' Tia asks me, breaking my thought.

'Yes. There will be me, Miriam, Dad and you at the front. Other assorted relatives and friends gathered around.'

'Is David coming?'

'He said he'd try. Sam Waterson wants to talk about a screenplay with him.'

'Can't he put her off?'

'It's Sam Waterson. He managed to get her to come an hour earlier. But still, traffic from the offices to here.'

'I guess.' I can hear a twinge of disappointment in her voice. 'What about Laura? Mum really liked her.'

Laura. I had not even realised that I would be thinking of Laura today, at least in the way I am, and her name stirs in my heart. 'I invited her. We're talking again. She said she'd try. But she has Natalie.'

'Natalie will be at the nursery. I called her too, she said she'd be here, but she wanted to check with you.'

'You talk to Laura?'

'All the time. I know it's not the time, but call her Will. Mum would want it.'

I feel that Tia's words are all at once emotional bribery and truth. I watch a bird fly across the cemetery, its wings beating furiously, carrying it higher into the grey skies. It is a cuckoo.

'It should be a good turnout,' I say. 'Dad says the W.I is coming.'

'That's nice of them.'

'It means we'll have a lot of cakes afterward in the hotel.'

'That'll please dad.' Tia answers, seemingly oblivious to the intended joke. 'If they've made Battenberg,' she adds, and I am glad that her humour is still with her.

The church is small, fourteen rows of chairs facing a raised pulpit. It feels odd standing in a building that Mum came to every weekend of her life, the place that I have come to celebrate and remember her in now. Dad and Miriam sit down, and I see him grip her hand tightly and lower his head. She whispers something into his ear, and he puts a hand onto her leg and pats it gently.

As Tia takes her seat, I glance back at the other mourners still filing into the building. I recognise many faces, and they all wear the same expressions of sadness and grief. A young boy looks bored, slightly angry at being forced to wear smart clothes and sit quietly. He sucks on a sweet. At the back of the church I see David. He waves discreetly, and I nod my head in direction. Then I realise I'm scanning the faces purposely, seeking out Laura's face amongst this crowd. But I do not see her.

Taking the seat next to Tia, I pick up a copy of the service plan and see Mum's face smiling back at me from a photograph I remember being taken at last year's Christmas festivities, when she got up and sang along with Songs of Praise on the television, and Tia bought her and Dad a holiday for two in France. They were supposed to take that trip this summer.

'It's a good brochure,' your father whispers to Tia, his wording seemingly inappropriate for the purpose of the plan he holds in front of him. 'Your Brian's a whiz on those computers. It's a good picture of her, don't you think?'

159

'It's lovely. She was lovely,' Tia answers, again wiping her eyes.

A hush falls over the church as Father John Williams enters and walks down towards his pulpit. He is an elderly man, his skin tight, blue veins traced on the back of his hands, and his white hair combed back and over, covering his increasing baldness. He looks out at the gathered, opens up a book that is in his hands.

'We are gathered here today to remember the life of Eileen Heather Hargreaves.' His voice is strong, with a distinct northern dialect. 'I have had the pleasure of knowing Eileen and her family, Geoff, Will and Tia for many years, and I do not need to tell those gathered here today in the presence of the Lord that she will be sadly missed. Though she will not be forgotten, for I know each of us will speak of her frequently. A great light has been dimmed on earth by her loss, but with our collective power we can keep that light alive.'

At the back of the church I hear someone offer their agreement with the statement, an 'amen' spoken quietly.

Examining the church more closely, taking in the ornate work on the stained glass, and at the intimacy of the surroundings, I begin to understand why Mum spoke so fondly of this place. I cannot imagine her wanting to be anyplace else.

I remember her eyes in those last few days. How they still looked around, trying to take in everything. Every little detail, trying not to miss anything, lest it become important later. I recall walking with her down a country path on a holiday in Wales, and she stopped to look at every bush and flower, and at every insect and bird, looking up into the canopy of leaves above us, finding the beauty in a raindrop or gasp of sunshine. 'Never close your eyes to the world William. You might miss something beautiful.'

Tia slides her hand onto mine, and I look at her, down to Dad who is crying into his handkerchief, and I smile sympathetically, as the tears run down my cheeks too.

The service continues, much of it becoming fogged in emotion, until all too quickly I realise it has ended and that I am standing with my sister. My legs feel like I have walked through treacle, the muscles seizing and aching, and it takes a moment to regain my senses.

As we emerge into the bright morning sunshine I see a gathering of people, talking quietly amongst themselves. Seeing us emerge, David comes walking over.

'None of us know where the hotel is.' He explains, and I tell him to follow my car.

Looking at the faces gathered I feel an overwhelming tide of gratitude that they have made the effort to be here with my family.

Then I see her face. Just for a moment, before someone blocks my view of her. I move away from Tia's arm, looking for another view of her, but I do not see her. Doubt begins to settle in my mind. Did I really see her? Or was it just my desire to see her creating the image of her face.

'Something wrong?' David asks. I had not realised he was still standing next to me.

'I just thought I saw something.' I look over at my father, 'let's get moving to the hotel, I don't think Dad can stand for much longer.'

David looks over at Dad too, and seeing his gait faltering, rushes to his side and slips an arm around my fathers, and the two of them begin to walk slowly towards the car, David listening tentatively to my father's words.

'He really is a good man.' Tia says.

'Always ready to help out.' I look at my friend, and my admiration for him swells. 'I should have invited Laura,' I say unexpectedly, even to myself. Tia stops and looks at me. 'Mum did like her.'

'Call her. Even if you don't really know what to say, she'll listen because it's you.'

161

'You're right. I think I need to talk to her now. I don't know why.'

I reach into my pocket and remove my mobile phone, find Laura's number and it rings twice before she answers. 'Hi Will,' she speaks, 'why are you calling me?'

'What do you mean?'

'I'm standing not less than a hundred metres from you. Turn around.'

I turn around, look down the pathway towards the main road, and see her, mobile phone in hand, dressed in a black suit. She gives a small wave and I hang up on the phone and slowly walk towards her. My heart beating in my chest, triple time.

Laura kisses me on the cheek, her hands tenderly holding my arms, and I know she is fighting within herself, trying not to kiss me on the lips. We both stand like that for a while, sun caressing us, morning breeze seeping across the grass.

'It was a good service.' She finally speaks. 'You did your mother proud in there.'

'Thank you,' I answer, wanting to talk about something other than the grief, and the loss. 'Where's Natalie?'

'With a sitter. I didn't want the risk of her disturbing the service. She's been getting so restless lately, so full of energy. I think she misses having you around.'

'It's strange. I find I miss her waking me up in the morning. I'd got used to her screaming, and crying and smiling. I never even thought.'

'I know it's not the right time to ask you this, but would you like to go for a drink with me some night. Just the two of us, we can talk, catch up.'

'Are you asking me out on a date?' For the first time in a few days a wry smile crosses my lips.

'I think I am.' Laura smiles too, and then we laugh. A deep, echoing laugh. A few mourners glance our way, appalled at our sudden expression of happiness.

I touch her hand, and look at the eyes of this woman, feeling my heart stirring, becoming saturated with love for her. In the corner of my eye I catch Tia smiling too, watching my every move.

The hotel has kindly provided us with the function room in which to hold the wake. When I finally enter the room a number of people have already gathered, congregated near to the small bar at which one young man is tending. Dad and Tia have already arrived and are sitting at a table, Miriam next to them, cradling a mug of coffee. I walk in, followed by David and Laura. Tia catches my eye and a brief smile crosses her lips.

'Would you come and sit with the family?' I ask David and Laura. 'Mum would want you too.'

'I need to go use the bathroom for a moment,' David quickly taps my arm and then disappears back down the corridor from which we've just come.

'Do you think he really needs the bathroom?' I ask Laura, conversation starters becoming fogged in my head, and the question I asked feels stupid.

'I think he's disappeared so we can have a moment to talk.' Laura says.

'Or do you think he just wants to cry in private?'

'Oh.' Laura blushes, embarrassed, and looks away. 'I didn't mean… It's just that….'

'I know we need to talk,' I reassure her. 'And we will do. I understand that now. What's been happening lately, it's shown me how much I need people that care about me, about how we can't always shut people away. You don't know how often I wanted to call you in the last few weeks, but I just couldn't.'

'I wanted to call you too, but I got scared as well. I wasn't even sure I should come today.'

'This is probably not the right time to ask this, or even to be thinking of it, but then again, maybe it is, I don't know. I don't think I know very much these days.'

'Just ask.' There is an almost pleading tone to her voice.

'This date of ours. Saturday night. I want this start as soon as we can. I want to be with you so much Laura. I want to do this properly this time.'

'We did it properly last time. Circumstance just got in the way. But let's not dwell over dead bones. Let's go sit with your family, that's what you need more than anything right now.'

She takes my hand in hers and begins to walk us over to the table. Dad looks up and sees the two of us, and I see the first glimmer of hope spreading across his face since he learnt how ill his wife was months ago. 'Thank you for coming Laura,' he says, 'You make Eileen and I very happy.' He stands up, his balance doddery, and kisses her on the cheek.

The number of guests at the wake bloats then thins out. Friends and relatives, some not spoken with for many months, and in some cases years, offer their commiserations, condolences and good wishes for the future, then drive away, to hotels and homes across the land. All the while the immediate family, David, Laura and a few other close friends stay gathered around the large central table of the dining room.

A few glasses of red wine lay strewn about, unfinished, and the conversation drifts around the remembrances of family holidays, amusing anecdotes and personal recollections of Mum. David, who seems to have fallen into the role of compere for the day, manages to control the mood successfully, and as I watch him, I am glad that he is here for us, that he is our friend.

A little later into the night, when people are standing, and ordering some food from the hotel restaurant, I approach David.

'I just want to thank you for coming today. It really means a lot.'

'I had to be here. When the great ones pass you should always be there.'

'I'm surprised you had the time. I know how busy we are at work right now.'

164

'I probably shouldn't admit this, but we probably lost a few clients today.' He pulls his mobile phone out of his trouser pocket. 'This is the first time this phone has been switched off since I don't even know when. I wouldn't have missed this. I had to be here for you.' I take my friend into a bear hug and hold him tightly for a few minutes. 'We're all going to miss her.'

I move into the hallway of the hotel, stopping to look at a painting of a typically English landscape when Laura walks up. She stands next to me in silence for a moment, two, looking at the painting as well.

'The girl at reception told me they are done by a local artist. He's getting famous apparently. Been on the BBC. About to have a show in London.'

'He's very talented.' I turn to look at her properly. 'How did we manage to get so tangled up?'

'What do you mean?'

'I think I've always walked away from things when the emotions got too intense. I've never been able to say what I really wanted to say.'

'What's bought this on?'

'Let's go sit down.'

The two of us walk through into the bar, which is still quiet. David, Tia, Miriam and Dad are sitting at a corner table and David waves to us as we enter. I point to Laura and indicate that I want to sit alone with her and he nods his head in understanding. I glance at the bar, undecided if I want a drink or not, and decide against it.

'Look at that,' Laura says, pointing up at the television set, which is on, but silent.

'What is it?'

'You don't recognise your own work? It's Doug's film, *Moonbeams Kiss the Sea*, the one we went to Brighton to see the filming of. The day we met.'

'I never saw it.' I look up at the television set for a moment, watching the film. 'Is it any good?'

'I never saw it either. Too many bad things happened around that time. I couldn't even face the premiere.'

'I'm sorry about that. You are right though, too many bad things did happen then. But they're over now.'

She smiles, agreeing.

'I've only ever loved four women in my life. My mother, Tia…' I look at Laura, 'You' she reaches across the table and squeezes my hand, 'and a girl called Sarah.'

'You've never mentioned a Sarah before.'

'I don't like to think about her. She was at university. A really beautiful young woman and I was crazy about her. The first women I loved. We were together for two and a half years. Most of our university days. Sarah Crowe. She was a singer, talented. Should have gone far.'

'What happened?'

'We went to this music festival in Devon. This really sleazy guy, in charge of record deals and all sorts, manipulated her. Made her do things. It wasn't her fault; she didn't want to do them. After that day she got really nervous about singing in public, it really knocked her for six. I sometimes look at the music presses; see if I can't see her name in some band, somewhere. But I haven't seen it. She must have given it up for good.'

'That's really sad.'

'And I really loved her. I knew she kissed some bloke at a party and I forgave her that. I wanted to forgive her for things that happened at the music festival but the words all got clogged in my throat, I couldn't talk, couldn't say what I needed to say.'

'What did you want to say to her?'

'I never told anybody this before in my whole life. I was going to ask her to marry me. That night in Devon.'

'So you broke up in Devon?'

166

'I walked away. Like I walked away from you on the night of the premiere. I shouldn't have done it with Sarah and I definitely shouldn't have done it with you. I get scared, I really get scared.'

Laura squeezes my hand very tightly. 'But we're getting back together. It's taken a while. I think we've needed that time to find the words to sort this all out. But you've found them now. I'm not giving up on you Will Hargreaves.'

I go to look at Laura straight in the eyes, but she looks away, and I feel a surge of rejection in my stomach. Then I realise she is looking at the television, 'Look Will. I'd forgotten.'

Laura points at the television set. I turn around and look at it properly, and my heart misses a beat. There, on the television screen, sit Laura and I, on Brighton beach, hands entwined, watching the sea. 'Remember? Doug said he put a surprise in the film for us,' Laura reminds me.

'The cheeky bugger. He filmed us.'

'He could see the feeling between us.'

And then almost as quickly as we were on screen, the scene changes, revealing Sam Waterson with her windswept, Bride of Frankenstein hair.

'That seems all so long ago.'

'Almost two years now.' Laura pronounces. 'Two years Will. We've been in and out of this for two years now.'

'So if we go off my record with women, in half a year I should be proposing to you. If I'm not running away.' I joke, laughing along with my own words and stirring memories.

'About Christmas day then. I look forward to it.' Laura replies, her voice earnest.

I look at her, at the strand of blonde hair hanging over her right eye, which she pushes away nonchalantly, at the deep blue of her eyes, and the whiteness of her skin, and her red lips. Her face seems alive with colour. I look at her and see the most beautiful woman I have ever seen. I look at her looking at me. I feel desire in my heart. I have not kissed this woman

167

passionately for months now, and I feel the sudden ache to take her in my arms.

And then I kiss her. Strongly. Feeling her tongue in my mouth and her fingers on my shoulders, pulling me in closer. My body charged with electricity.

'So are you and Laura back together?' David asks, eagerly, cornering me beside the bar. Tia is standing next to him, pretending to be less interested, but still leaning in closely.

'David, did you know Laura and I were in Doug's film?'

'What?' He exclaims, 'What's that got to do with anything? Of course I knew. But what about you and Laura? Are you back together?'

'We're going on a date on Saturday. But taking things slow." David smiles. He goes to ask a question. 'I know you want the juicy details, but not now David. Ok. It's not the time to talk about these things."

'But Will. That's the thing. It is. Your mother really cared about Laura, and the two of you getting back together will make her passing into Heaven more beautiful, because you, her son, are back with the woman we all know you should be with.'

'That was almost beautiful David,' Tia says.

'I always had this natural urge towards the poetic,' he minces, 'but you know I only said it to get all the juicy gossip out of Mr Shyness here.' David throws an arm around me. 'Seriously, and I know I'm often not, so this tells I what I'm about to say is important, you and Laura, back together, fucking brilliant. You and Laura working towards building a strong relationship, it proves there's hope for us all. Your mother's smiling down on us all right now – that's why I'm still in the suit – don't want God to see me in my slacks, he wouldn't let me in! – and she's wanting nothing more than to see the two of you work.'

I look at my friend and my sister, then over at Laura who is talking quietly with my father. This is my family.

'I don't know if I say this enough David, but I love you. And you're a bastard for not telling either us that we were in Doug's film.'

'I love you both too.' He pulls me and Tia in close. 'We're damn lucky to know each other. And you Will Hargreaves, I wanna hear from you 9am Sunday morning, with every juicy piece of gossip.' He laughs, pulling us both in closer, the barman throwing us a strange glance, then returning to drying a glass.

PART FIVE

AFTER-LIFE
MID 1998

1.

Thursday

The rain poured in rivers down the windowpane as I sat watching the morning traffic from the front window of my home. It had been twenty-four weeks since Mum died, twenty four weeks since I asked Laura out once again, bringing her back into my life once more. This time I had chosen to do things slower, rightly. She and Natalie lived in a small flat, and though we saw each other in the offices of Riverbank every weekday, we were treating the romance as something that existed only outside office hours, not wanting the ferocity of emotion to overwhelm us in our business lives. Despite that we still spent every weekend in each other's company, and even a few long nights after a day's work.

David kept his watchful eye on us both, talking to us both individually, learning when we were together that he said the same thing to us both, 'You're doing well so far, don't screw this up.' He told me every person in the office was behind us both.

Tia phoned me every other night for the first few weeks. She wanted to know the details, the minutiae of our dates, about what was said and what was not said. She confessed she spoke to Laura about it too, on a few lunch dates they had in some chic south Kensington café. Dad said our relationship reminded him of when he was courting his wife, of those early days in Cambridge when he walked with her along the banks of the Cam, through the parks, hands entwined and they talked about everything and about nothing, and their love just grew surely and steadily.

This time it felt special. That was what surprised me the most. That there was still that strange, glowing sense of this being special, of this being something more than any of the others. We had been doing new strange things – writing letters to one another, letters that made this relationship feel strengthened, deepened, curiously coy, twee, but beautiful. I felt a sense of being a giddy teenager in love, a fifties love song come to life. Only her letters were strong, passionate, full of feeling, telling secrets she shared with no one else. She spoke in a language I was afraid of using, words that secreted themselves inside my heart and blossomed there, making each intimate contact that followed more effervescent.

I tried to imitate her phrases, her turn of words, but she giggled at them, playfully, and told me just say what I would normally say, that I should just be myself. She seemed to be under my skin. It was great.

Tracing my finger down the windowpane, following a bead of rain, I could see David's car pulling up outside, so grabbing my coat I emerged from the warmth of the house into the cold December rains, arms wrapped around my body, trying to retain the heat. What is happening now frightens me. I am ashamed of the secret I am keeping.

2.

Tia is waiting for me in the entrance to the school when I pull up in my car. She waves to draw attention to herself.

'I didn't think the teachers were allowed to skip class as well.' I joke as she climbs into the passenger seat.

'Once in a while. So where are we going? Someplace special I hope.'

'For you sis, always. When have I ever let you down?'

'Do you really want me to repeat that list?'

'Good point.'

I exit the school grounds, and turn onto the main road, heading out of town.

The city streets narrow out slowly as we pass through the greenbelt into the countryside. The radio is playing quietly in the back, the front speakers muted so the two of us can talk if we wish, but not so there is this unearthly quiet if we wish not to. Tia is resting her head against the headrest, eyes closed, but I know she is not sleeping, just contemplating the things that shall have to be done.

'Are you sure this is what Daddy wants?' She asks me, disturbing my own thoughts. Her question takes a second to process in my mind, and I realise I had been thinking the same.

'He's getting on now. After Mum's passing he's getting scared. He's out in the country, and yeah the neighbours are good, they keep watch on him, but what if he falls in the night, nobody would find him till morning.'

'Isn't it the same in London though? Worse so, maybe. He's not going into a home, he's moving into a flat. We're closer to him, but we're not there all night.'

'We can get a panic button installed. They do that. David's mother has one.'

'But she presses it when she needs a cup of tea!'

The two of us laughed, the humour relieving some of the festering concern.

'If this doesn't work,' I carry on, 'then there are other alternatives. I'd just not like to think of them at this juncture.'

'I don't think Daddy would take kindly to us thinking of them either.'

Dad is sitting in a garden chair, his newspaper spread out over the plastic table, its edges weighted down with stones at either end. He does not look up as I open the car doors, and step out of the vehicle. It is only when Tia calls out, 'good morning Daddy,' that he realises we have arrived.

'I'll be with you in a moment,' he calls back; 'I just want to finish reading this article on European sex slaves.'

'European sex slaves?' Tia mutters, 'what *is* he reading? Don't tell me he's started buying a tabloid paper now.'

'You've got to allow him some excitement. At least he's not reading about the lives of soap stars yet. At least I hope not.'

Tia pushes open the garden gate, and indicates for me to enter. I take a seat on the other side of the table to Dad, and Tia sits between us, glancing over at the paper that he is reading. '*The Daily Mirror*? You can do better than that, surely?'

'Your mother started me reading it. We like all the gossip. Who really wants to read about Tony Blair's latest foreign policy?'

It is strange hearing Dad saying these things; they seem somehow at odds with the view of him that I carry around in my head. It also makes me wonder what I actually know about him, and about the life he leads.

He asks if I would like anything to drink, and Tia offers to go and get a mug of tea for each of us. She stands, and disappears into the house.

'It's good weather today. You wouldn't think it was near Christmas.'

'Not at all,' I say, stepping through the obligatory small talk with him. 'It's almost summer-like. Mind, they say this heat wave isn't going to last.'

'It never does. I'm beginning to think I should move to the south of France. A lot of people my age are doing it these days. Just packing up and leaving for the Dordogne.'

'Like who?'

'Frank. You remember Frank? He bought a maisonette in Lyon. Half the price of houses around here and he has a swimming pool. Imagine it, having a swimming pool. It would do my hips wonders, I'm sure of it.'

'You wouldn't know anybody, though. Wouldn't it get lonely?' Dad shoots me a look that I interpret as being *I don't care about that*, 'and besides Dad, you don't speak French.'

'That doesn't matter these days. The continent is full of Englishmen now. I saw it on TV. There are more Englishmen over there than there are French men.'

'Somehow I don't believe that Dad.'

'You could come visit. Bring Laura. I'm sure the two of you would love to have a holiday villa. You could come stay for a long weekend sometimes.'

'Maybe. We haven't taken a holiday together yet.'

'Not even a dirty weekend to some rural hotel?'

'Well… I don't think the issue is whether Laura and I want somewhere we could visit in France.'

'It'd make an old man happy.'

'I'm sure.'

'Laura would like it too. I asked her the other day.'

'You spoke to Laura?'

'She's a lovely woman. We all like her.'

I laugh, 'sometimes it seems my family talk to my girlfriend more than I do.' And Dad laughs with me too.

'When are you going to propose to her son?'

'I don't know. We're taking it slow.'

'If you take it too slow she might get bored.'

'I doubt it Dad. We love each other. It's enough right now.'

'It's what she wants Will. I'm sure of it. No other woman has been so patient with you.'

'Can we not talk about my relationship history?'

'But Will,' I hear Tia's voice, and see her coming out of the house carrying a tray with three mugs of tea on, 'that's our favourite topic.' She puts the try down and laughs, rubbing my shoulder playfully.

The three of us sit in silence for a few moments, watching another elderly gentleman ambling down the street, an excitable terrier running circles around his feet, the man's protestations to stop falling on uninterested ears.

'So what brings you two down here today? It's not often I see you together these days.' Tia looks at me, anxious, not really wanting to endure this conversation. 'What is it?' Dad asks, his love for his children enabling him to read our thoughts.

I look at him, at his hollowing, fragile eyes. I feel I am dragging him into shadow lands of hurt, of uncertainty. The idea seems absurd now, that I could ever wish to take him away from everything he loves, everything that has given him purpose in these, the twilight years of his life. I wish I could buy him that villa in France.

'We're worried about you Dad.' I finally say.

'Worried? What have you got to be worried about? I'm doing just fine out here. Jill, from number seven, comes and checks on me periodically. I can still cook, climb stairs. I walk a mile to the paper shop and back every day. When was the last time you walked a mile?' Tia lowers her head; a rush of guilt overwhelms me. Dad looks at us both, picks up his mug of tea and goes to take a sip but places it back down on the table. 'You think I'm ready for a home? You're ready to lock me up and throw away the key.'

'Nobody's said home Daddy.' Tia interrupts. 'We're not talking about a home.'

'So what are we talking about?'

'A flat. In London.' I say. 'Between Tia and myself. We can see you more often, and if anything should happen, Heaven forbid, then we can get there quicker. When Mum was ill it took me an hour just to get here. That's not right. Anything can happen in an hour.'

'So we're doing this to ease your pains, rather than for my benefit?'

'You're twisting our words Daddy.'

He shoots me an acidic glance, then stands up and begins to walk towards the house, but stops and turns to face us both. 'As a parent,' he begins, 'something neither of you understand yet, you know that one day this is going to happen. That you're going to become a burden. That your children are going to want to move you, take you away from everything you love, so they can try and give you more love. All my life I've dreaded the day you come to me and say, 'we think you need to be put in a home.' I dreaded it more than I did losing your mother, because selfishly I always thought I would be the first to die. I've lost so much in these last years, my wife has gone, my best friends are passing on, or being moved to homes too. There's no worse indignity than having to live out your twilight years in sterile white corridors, being tended to every five seconds. I'm not leaving this home. Your mother and I always said we wanted to die here, and die here I will.'

Tia goes to speak but his looks says *don't say a word*, so she looks away as Dad turns back around and storms into the house, slamming the door behind him. Tia looks at me pleadingly, confusedly and with tears welling in her eyes. I just look down at the ground, silenced.

As the air chills, the sun sinking behind grey clouds, Tia places Dad's newspaper on the same tray as the mugs of tea, and stands.

'We can't stay out here all afternoon; we've got to face him sometime. He's had time to cool and we've had time to think. We should go in.'

I nod in agreement, and stand too. At the front door, Tia indicates for me to enter first, and I understand her apprehension. I push open the door, and hear the sound of the television, and head towards the living room. I recognise the sounds as being a quiz show, though I do not know which one, but as I push open the living room door Dad switches the television off.

'You don't have to do that, watch the end if you want.'

'I've seen it before. They repeat too much these days.' He pauses, looks down at the table, 'I wondered how long it would be before you came in for a second push.'

'We're not forcing you Dad. This was supposed to be a discussion.'

He lets a brief smile cross his lips. 'I got that wrong, didn't I? I was never very good at knowing when people had the best intentions.' I am not sure what he means. 'I think when your mother said she wanted to die in this house; she meant she wanted to die wherever I was.' I sit down opposite him and lean forward on the chair. Tia enters the room and leans back against the wall, slightly out of his field of vision. 'I have a lot of memories with her in this house, but I have been doing some thinking. Maybe you're right. Maybe it is time to move. And maybe it's not. If I move to London, I want it to be something I choose to do. To a place I choose. I will come with you and look at properties. I'm not promising anything. And I know that all the time I'm out here you'll worry about me, but I have to know it is the right thing to do.'

'Tia and I found a place that might suit you.'

'I hate it already. I will choose somewhere, not either of you.'

'Did anybody ever tell you that you're a stubborn bastard sometimes?'

'All the time,' and he laughs, deep and booming, falling back into his seat. I look at Tia, then back at him, and begin to laugh as well. 'Now come on,' he finally speaks again, 'The Eastenders omnibus is on a bit, let's watch it together.'

'You were saying something about soap stars earlier Tia?' I say to my sister, and she shakes her head in mock desperation and takes a seat next to Dad, throwing an arm around his neck and cuddling in close, still his little girl.

Dad turns the television off and looks at us, his children, and I look back, a sense of welcome filtering through the room.

'Now are you two running back to the city or are you going to stay with me and eat. I have some beef cutlets that need eating.'

'You don't have to ask us to stay Daddy. Of course we'll stay. Why don't the two of you stay here, chat, and I'll see to the food.'

Tia leaves the living room. I look at Dad, at his greyed hair and at the way he is slumped in his chair, his shoulders heavy.

'Is this where the third attack begins?' He asks, a slight smile crossing his face, though the look makes me suspect that it might not just be a joke.

'We should come out to see you more often. I'd not thought about it, but I don't come and see you in person enough. The telephone makes everything so much easier, but it takes away the intimacy.'

'What are you talking about son? You don't need to feel guilty. It's the way things develop between families. It works the other way too, there's nothing to say I couldn't have come to visit you.'

I want to say something but I am not sure what.

'I've wanted to come down to London,' he carries on, 'see you and Tia. Laura tells me I should come and visit you. Did she tell you Natalie asked about me?'

'She did. I didn't think Natalie would have been old enough to remember you.'

'Kids are intelligent Will, more than you probably give them credit for. I don't think you realise it until you have children of your own.' He takes a moment, 'Do you think you'll have kids with Laura?'

His questions hits me like a hammer, unexpected, thought provoking. I look away from him, something inside of me fleeing from the notion, though if I were truthful I would admit to having thoughts of it.

'I don't know Dad.' I feel awkward. 'That's something that's way off. If at all.'

'You've been together over two years.'

'Erratically so at times.'

'But still together. Over two years Will, it's a commitment to someone; even if you don't want to see it as such. You've only been with one woman as long, and we all know how serious you were about her. And you were only a child then, really.'

'I was twenty.'

'Merely a child in terms of relationships. You don't stay with someone for two years if you don't love them. You even moved in with Laura for a while. It's time you stopped running away from the idea of commitment. You have a gorgeous woman that loves you, and that you love too.'

'I know that Dad.'

182

'I don't think you do. Your mother always said that we'd have wait for you to get married. That your sister would marry first, and the way she's going with Brian, it might even be within the year. And they were off and on too.'

'Tia's different Dad.'

'Yes, she is. She has her head screwed on properly.' I feel belittled by my father, and I shrink a little in my chair. 'Now, instead of trying to sort my life out, why don't you go outside, call Laura and ask her out for a meal.'

I stand up, walk towards the door, then turn and look at my father, 'How long did you and Mum date before getting engaged?'

'Seven years. But things were different back then.'

'Seven years. When were you sure she was the one?'

'From the moment I saw her.'

Laura's mobile phone clicks into answer phone, and I stand in Dad's garden for a moment watching a young boy pedalling down the street on his tricycle, legs turning furiously on the pedals, rushing towards uncertainty with zeal.

'Just at my Dad's, thought I'd call you. I'll phone later tonight. Love you. Will. I do love you Laura. Shit. I wish this wasn't answer phone. I'll call you very soon. Bye.'

Tia and Dad look at me expectantly as I re-enter the living room.

'Did you speak to her?' Tia fails to hide her excitement.

'Answer-phone,' I say, dejected.

'At least you called.' Dad tries to proffer comfort.

'I know what I've got to do, though. And I know how to do it.'

'And what's that?'

'You'll find out. Dad, look, about moving, just come look at London, if you don't like it, well this is only an hour drive.'

183

He looks at me, figuring out what I mean, and then a wicked smile of conspiracy flashes across his face. 'Sometimes I think you're completely insane. You must get that from me. And sometimes I think you're the cleverest man on earth. You get that from your mother. Good luck son. Not that you'll need it.'

'What are you going to do?' Tia asks me, still not in on the secret.

'I'm going to ask Laura to marry me.'

Tia is sitting next to me in the car, as we cruise along the empty motorway back down towards London. I left Dad twenty minutes ago, but instead of driving the direct route home, I am taking a more leisurely path home, wishing to have some more time to speak with Tia about the events of the afternoon. Instead of talking, however, we are sitting in silence, the initial over-excitement having slipped into quiet contemplation. I keep my eyes on the road, a Harold Melvin CD playing quietly in the background, the notes whispering out quietly, seductively. I reach over to the volume control and turn it up. Tia glances at me, but then turns back to watch the road too.

'This shouldn't feel like a bad time,' Tia finally speaks, quietly, and I just about make out her words. 'You just told us you're going to propose. That should feel good.'

'It does,' I try and explain. 'But what if it goes wrong? What if she says no?'

'She won't. We all know Laura; we know how she feels about you. If she says no, well then we can only assume we didn't know her at all. But we know her. And I know she'll say yes.'

I do not know what it is I want to say. Tia reaches over and turns the music off.

'I can see you're scared Will, and I think I know why. At Mum's funeral, you talked to Laura about an ex-girlfriend. When I saw her next she told me about it, about how she could tell you had been really hurt by this girl, and that it was affecting

184

your relationships even now. I spoke to Daddy about her. Sarah was her name, right?' I nod my head. 'You never told me you wanted to propose to another woman before, and I understand why. But that was all such a long time ago, with a different woman in a different time. Laura isn't Sarah. Laura loves you dearly; she's not going to hurt you like that.'

'I know that. I can see that.'

'But?'

I want to laugh. Laugh in the knowledge that Tia knows me so well. In the understanding that my life is changing before my very eyes and I can see it happening. That everything that has happened has brought me to this.

'I'm scared Tia. Scared in a way I've never felt before. It's like every fibre of my body is shaking. I just want to be with her now.'

Tia lets out a gentle laugh, 'seems my big brother's finally grown up.'

'This is a big thing. Perhaps the biggest I'll ever do. Now I've got to make sure I do it right. I don't want it screwed up.'

'And how will that happen? It can't.'

'It can Tia. With Sarah, I just walked away when I should have stayed with her and worked through the issues. With Liz, or Jane, or hell even Rosy... they were relationships where I fucked it up through some stupidity of my own. I've almost messed this one up too many times now.'

'But she's still with you. And you've said it yourself; this one is different to all of them. Take Jane, how long were you with her? Five months? Six? You've been with Laura for getting close to three years now. Like Daddy said, you love her and she loves you.' I go to speak, 'and don't say 'I know' again, because sometimes I wonder if you do. We shouldn't even have to have this conversation. All you do is buy a ring, book a table at an expensive restaurant, get down on one knee and ask her to marry you. It's not rocket science.'

I think for a moment about her words, watching carefully as a van changes lanes ahead of us. 'Are you waiting for Brian to propose? How does that feel?'

'We've talked about it. I know he will soon. I don't know how I know – woman's intuition, probably.'

'Probably.'

'Watch it! You're still not too big to beat up.'

'Like you could ever take me!'

Tia laughs, 'I always went easy on you. We all know how sensitive you can be.'

'Seriously, though, you know Brian is the one?'

'I do.'

'How much torture is it waiting for that moment when he asks you?'

'I always thought it would be worse than it is. It's terribly exciting, nerve-wracking, and painful. But still, despite that, I know he will, and I love him, so I'm patient. And because I'm patient, I'm sure of him. Let me ask you a question – when did you first think of proposing to Laura?'

'Not long after I met her. Dad said he knew the first day when it came to Mum.'

'And so will you in twenty years. So will Brian. Once it's all happened, I think we let the romantic eyes take over, and the past becomes rosier than it ever really was. Your break with Laura, that whole time, that'll become something else.'

'Do you know,' I interrupt Tia, 'I've just thought of something.'

'What's that?'

'Well if Brian proposes soon, the two of us may well end up marrying around the same day.'

'Well there's a thought.'

'Isn't it. And I just had another. I know where I'm going to propose.'

I drop Tia off at her flat, and she invites me in for a quick drink with Brian, but I politely decline, knowing that there are certain things that I want to get worked out in my head, that there are things going on that will influence everything else that happens hereafter.

Pulling out into her street, and stopping briefly at the intersection, I hit the answer phone button on my mobile phone, which I had noticed flashing earlier in the afternoon. There is a moment's silence, and I press the button to hear the messages.

'Hi Will,' I hear Laura's voice filling the cocoon, 'just got your message. Thanks. I love you too. I'm guessing things aren't quite going according to plan at your Dad's. Give me a call when you're back in the city, I can come round. I'm up till late, got to finish this proposal for David, and could do with a break. It'd be lovely to see you. Natalie's asleep now, thank God. She wouldn't settle earlier. I wrote you another letter today, you'll get that tomorrow. Anyway, give us a call, come round, love you. Bye.' And then there is the crackle at the end of the message, and without even thinking about it I change the direction in which I'm heading, so that I can go see Laura instead. I decide to surprise her, and part of me cannot wait to see her face, the look of surprise spreading over her, and the smile that she will give me when I arrive.

And then the answer phone kicks in with a second message. 'This is Doctor Rajiv Patel, needing to leave a message for William Hargreaves. We have an appointment come available, two days from now at nine in the morning. If you could call us back and confirm that you can take it, then I shall see you then. Goodbye.'

I had forgotten about that. That all that had happened recently had led me to this. That those first traces of blood in my throat, glistening against the white porcelain of the bathroom sink, had made me not think of my own health, but of my fathers. That I called him up on the telephone and talked for the longest time, then to my sister, and I collaborated to bring him to London, closer to my home. Perhaps in a way I knew the truth then, even if it had not dawned in consciousness.

Then the next morning this journey finally began.

Arriving at Laura's house, I manage to park near to her front door, and after locking the car, walk up the steps to her home. Ringing the doorbell it seems like an inordinate amount of time before she arrives. Her face brightens seeing me, and she throws her arms around me.

'I knew you wouldn't call,' she says, 'You like the spontaneity too much.'

I smile and kiss her, and she leads me into the flat, closing the door behind her as she does.

'I'm glad you've come around. I've been thinking about you all day.'

'Me too,' I say in what sounds like a dull response, but Laura kisses me again, harder than before.

'Did it go well at your Dad's?' She asks.

'It didn't go the way I planned. But it's given me a lot to think about.'

'And what does that mean? You're being overly cryptic again.'

'It means I think things are moving in the right direction.' Sitting down on her sofa, she nestles her head in my lap and looks up at me. I stroke her hair. 'I have something that needs to be done on Thursday. I need to be driven there and picked up.'

'David'll give me the time off to do that.'

'I want David to take me there, but I want you to pick me up.'

'Sure,' she agrees, 'what's up?'

'I don't know yet.' I smile at her, fingers running through her hair, her blue eyes radiating concern and love towards me. 'You know you're the most beautiful woman I've ever met.'

She blushes, eyes glancing away for a second. 'Flattery will get you everywhere tonight,' and she reaches up and cradles my face, 'You're different tonight. It's like something burdening you has been taken away. Like you're getting ready for the next phase of something important.'

'You don't know how right you are.'

'What is going on Will?'

'All in the right time. I'm not hiding anything because I don't know yet. But don't worry, when I know you'll be the first person I tell.'

Laura leans up and kisses me on the lips, 'it's only because I know you and love you that I'll walk blindly with you. I've learnt you always say what needs to be said, even if it takes you a while. Now come on, let's go to bed, and leave all this in the shelter of the night, for another night, when things become clearer.'

Laura stands and taking my hand leads me down the corridor towards her bedroom. I stop for a moment, and push open the door to Natalie's room. Shards of light cross her face as she sleeps soundly. Laura eases next to me and slips her arm around my waist, and the two of us stand there for a moment, watching her child sleep, while outside the world carries on, everything oblivious to everything else. The snake turning in my chest, coiling with uncertain ferocity.

Laura kisses my cheek, 'how did I ever end up with a man so good?'

3.

Thursday Again

'I've just got to post this letter,' I say to David as I climb into his car. 'The post-box is at the end of the street.'

'Another one of your love letters to Laura?'

'Something like that.'

'So where are we going Will? It's not often you call me in the early hours of a day and say you need to be driven somewhere.'

'I need to go to the hospital David.'

'Why? What's wrong?' I hear the immediate concern in my friends' voice.

'Nothing's wrong. My car's off the road, and I have to go visit someone there.'

'Really?' I can hear the disbelief in his voice, and not without good reason I know.

'Really,' I try and sound more convincing.

'OK then,' he says, 'the hospital to visit your friend it is.'

'You don't have to drive me back. I've got that covered.'

David shoots a look my way, then back onto the road. I wish I could tell him, but once again the words get stuck in my throat.

'So what do you write in all these letters? They've become something of an office mystery. Shelley in finances is willing to pay good money to see what you write.'

'They're private. No bidder, no matter how much money, will ever get to see them. I wouldn't show them to anybody. Not even you. Not even Tia.'

'But what do you talk about in them?'

'Life, dreams, our relationship. They're dull to anybody else.'

'But that's the good stuff. You just don't get it, do you?'

'You're not reading them.'

'Bastard.'

'I know.' And the two of us laugh.

David eases the car to a stop outside the hospital. He grips the steering wheel and looks at me, and I see the concern his eyes. He knows that there is something I am not telling him. I have to give him credit for his intuitiveness.

'Are you sure you don't need me to pick you up?'

'I'm sure. I'll see you at the office tomorrow.'

'You don't have to come in if you don't feel like it.'

'There's nothing wrong with me David. I'll see you tomorrow.'

'Can't a friend get worried?'

'God, you're like a nagging wife!' I clamber out of the passenger seat, and then lean back into the car through the open window. 'And that's why you're a good friend. See you tomorrow.'

He proffers his hand, and I grip it tightly. 'I know I don't need to say this, but if you want to talk.'

I nod my head in understanding. David looks at me for a second, and then I step away from the car and he drives off, leaving me standing in the cold air before I enter the hospital, a surge of bile rising and sinking in my throat.

The metallic hum of engines working behind the sterile white cocoon of the M.R.I machine into which they have me reminds me of being underwater and trying to hear my sister talking. Of being in the isolation tank, only here I cannot escape reality. There is an uneasy compression over my ears, and my eyes, which are closed, see only a swirling inky black.

I try and concentrate on other things, and those things that would make this process quicker, easier to understand. I imagine Laura's face, as I saw it last night in candlelight, in a small Kensington restaurant. As the two of us sat, me playing with her fingers across the table, and listening to a string quartet playing quietly in the corner, just watching one another, drinking in every detail, not wishing to speak, for any sound may shatter the beauty.

The sound of the machine turning around intrudes on my thoughts, however, and the remembrance of being in a hospital, of blood spewing from my lips over the bathroom sink a few weeks ago, and of the uncertainties come flooding back, like unwanted things.

Electric lights blind as the M.R.I machine finishes working and I emerge into the cold, white room. I close my eyes again, trying to force the light away, and a crackled mechanical voice tells me I can sit up now, that the examination is over. A young nurse comes across and offers me a glass of water. Everything at this moment feels blank.

Standing on the street corner outside the hospital I take out my mobile phone and select Laura's name from the memory. She answers after two rings.

'Hi Laura, are you in work?' I ask her.

Her voice is distorted by a poor mobile phone line, 'You're early.'

'I know. Can you come and pick me up now?'

'Yeah. You are alright, aren't you Will?'

'I'm fine. It was just a check up. See you soon,' and I hang up before she has any chance to ask further questions, preferring to deal with them in person.

I see Laura's car coming up the road beside the hospital and flag her down. Instead of waiting outside the hospital doors as I agreed, I have wandered down out of the grounds, wanting to get away from that stench of illness and death.

She stops the car and I slide into the passenger seat, and then pulling back into the busy street we sit in silence. I can see questions flickering openly across Laura's face, but I am not yet ready to say what I need to say, and I appreciate her allowing me the patience to do this in my own time.

Up ahead I see road works, the noise of a pneumatic drill piercing the otherwise quiet afternoon air, smoke and concrete being blasted. We stop at the red light, and I look away, still feeling uncertain of the words.

'David said I didn't need to come back today,' Laura finally breaks the disquiet, 'we can go have an early meal somewhere, if you want?'

'I don't feel much like eating at the moment. But if you're hungry?'

'I just don't know where we're going. You haven't said. And even though I don't mind driving around with you, we have to have a destination.'

'How about Cambridge?'

'Cambridge?'

'Yeah. Why not? Phone Carol, I'm sure she won't mind looking after Natalie for a few more hours.'

'I suppose...'

'And I know a great restaurant there; it'll give me the time I need to figure out what to say.'

'What's wrong Will?'

But before I get a chance to answer, or even bluff my way out of answering the red light flashes to green, and Laura's driving

194

once more, concentrating on finding her way through the chaotic city streets.

'Call Carol then. Cambridge it is.' She finally says, and before long we're heading out of the city, headed north, back to the beginning.

'How bad?'
'The cancer is spreading.'
'How long?'
'It's not an exact science Will.'
'How long?'
'Soon,' he says, 'soon.'

Laura taps my shoulder, waking me from restless sleep, and as I open my eyes I fail to recognise the street in which we're parked.

'We're here, in Cambridge. I didn't know where you wanted to go, so I stopped here.'

'We're not in the city centre?'

'Not yet, in the outskirts somewhere, you're going to have to direct me.' She starts the car engine, 'I had a phone call from the hospital while you were sleeping. They want you to come in on Monday at nine to see a doctor. Raj Pavel? Something like that. They said you'd know.'

'Rajiv Patel. I know. Let's just follow the signs for the city centre, and find somewhere to park.'

Laura pulls back into the light traffic. 'What are we doing here Will? I'm getting a little worried. What's going on?'

'I'll tell you soon.'

She drives in silence for a short while until we are in the city centre, and I lead her down a small side street, before heading down a small flight of steps to the pathway along the Cam, onto the paths I once knew so well. Walking hand in hand, I talk for a while about the minor and trivial things – the latest script that Riverbank are producing, about taking David and Doug out for a meal to celebrate their six month anniversary of the last six month anniversary of getting together, about taking Natalie to Longleat – then we arrive at a small pub in the middle of one of the lawns that encroach on the banks.

Ordering a glass of red wine and a pint of beer, I find a quiet corner, close to the crackling fire, and Laura reaches across the table and holds my hand.

'Are you ready yet to tell me what this is all about?'

'We've been together two and a half years now. You're my longest relationship. The best relationship I've ever been in. You're my best friend.'

Laura squeezes my hand and smiles deeply, 'I know.'

'I have to tell you something, I came here tonight to propose to you, but...'

Her mouth falls open; she misses a breath, her words filling the second gap between your words... '...I accept...'

'...I think I've got cancer.'

Her mouth drops lower, her hands shake for a moment. Her lips tremble, her eyes widen, and then shrink, tears gathering in the corners.

'I love you Laura. I want you to be my wife. I know you'll marry me. But that phone call. Rajiv Patel. They sent me for tests to see if I have cancer. He's called back so quickly... I don't know though.'

I can see she is lost for words.

'I wasn't going to mention it now, not until I knew.'

'It's not certain yet?'

'They haven't said it is.'

'Then we don't need to worry.'

'Sometimes you just know.'

She searches for words to say but tears just streak from her eyes.

'This wasn't meant to happen like this. We're going to fight this. I've got the best medical help. We'll be fine. If I have you at my side that's half the battle won.'

'I won't leave you. I'll never leave your side.' I hear notes of determination in her voice, and am glad for that. 'David will stand by you. We'll all stand beside you. You're only young. You can beat this.'

'I hope.'

'You will. For me. For our future children. You will. I want to live with you and our two children by the sea.'

'Our future children? So we're going to have children are we?' I try and make a small joke through the tears.

'At least two.'

I take a long drink of beer, and look directly at Laura. 'Will you marry me?'

PART SIX

WHEN THE RAINS FALL

EARLY 1999

1.

The screech of a car horn startles me from slumber. My eyes jump awake, light shattering my corneas, pupils protracting, dilating. I slam my eyelids shut and try and drown out the cacophony outside the hotel window. The net curtains swaying as if to a tango, the wall and the air unwilling partners. I open my eyes again and lift the tumbler of water off the side cabinet and drink the liquid, the liquid that dampens my mouth, soothing the bristles that have grown in my throat over night. It is a new day in Cambridge. The air is humming with the threat of a storm; there is that pressure, that smell of nature's tension. I look at the numbers on my digital watch and the seconds changing seem like knifes stabbing me. I drop the watch to the ground and roll over on the bed.

I wonder if this hotel serves breakfast, and at what time. I cannot remember asking them when I checked in late last night. Then I realise I do not want any food, that my stomach, though empty, needs no filling. 'Soon,' I hear Doc Patel saying, and I rub my hand against my ear to silence his words.

Then I try and recall why I am here, why I have come to this city at this time. It made sense to drive here yesterday, but now that that day has faded like linen left in the sun too long, it is lost to me.

I shower slowly, letting the force of the water vibrate against my skin, droplets repelled, splashing the wall and seeping over onto the floor outside the cubicle. This hotel seems to be falling apart at the seams. At any time I expect to see a cockroach, like in some bad American movie.

Rubbing the condensation from the mirror, I look at myself for what feels like the first time. I see the cloud of stubble on my face and the hairs on my chest, black and sodden, and my sex, unerect and flabby. I feel no need for sex ever again, the thought of it echoes hollow in my mind. I think of Laura, sitting in her new apartment with Natalie, and I think of the first time she touched me, and how that was the best sex I had ever had. I close my eyes and I can see her naked now, that she looks incredibly beautiful, and I think of all those wonderful memories. And then I dress and walk out into the streets of Cambridge, banishing all those thoughts from my mind. I cross a bridge, and then cut down onto the path along the Cam that I recall leads into the City Centre. Other than that, I do not know where I am going. And that feels right. Somehow.

Cambridge is quiet on this Tuesday morning. A few people are wandering around the shops. I hear a snatch of conversation as a couple walk past me, '...Robson Green's shooting a movie by the...' but it all seems wasteful. Everything seems wasteful, just dead air floating away from their lives. I walk past the coffee shop where Sarah used to work when we were students here, though the façade has changed – the fading yellows now false wooden panelling, the name now longer something quaintly English but something French. I remember kissing her in the alleyway beside the shop. That long night, after the rains had fallen after our first fight, and the street glistening, shimmering orange with reflections of street lights, and her mascara running with her tears and my lips touching hers, trying to reassure her that things would be getting better.

I walk on down the street, past one of the many bookshops, and bistros, cafes and faceless high street stores, and for a moment I feel as if I am back there, in my university days. But the city seemed different then. Back then it had life, and now it feels empty, crass. Part of me feels as if this is how it should be, though another part of me knows that my experiencing of this city right now is simply because of how things are, that right now, at this moment in my life, I hate life. Hate it for giving me what it has, for dealing me this hand.

I feel nauseous. Finding a small café, with few people in, I take a seat near the back. It is a quiet place. The tables are adorned with light blue table cloths, a small vase with fresh flowers, and the usual condiments of such establishments. I pick up their menu but do not read what is written there. When a young waitress approaches, I instinctively know she is a student at the university – even after all this time I still recognise the expressions – and I order a coffee, milky. She scribbles my order and asks me if I would like anything else, when I become aware of another body coming towards the table. For a second I wonder if there is some sign saying 'talk to me, I need to talk' or if they think I am Robson Green. Then I recognise the eyes, I have seen them looking at me before.

'It can't be,' that familiar female voice says, 'Will Hargreaves?'

'Hello Egg.'

2.

'Long time no see,' Egg says, taking the seat opposite without being asked. 'How the hell are you?'

'I'm OK,' I lie.

'What brings you back here? Not working on a film are you? Any chance of a part?' She smiles at me, fake and mockingly.

'How did you know I work in films?'

'Sarah said she saw your name in the credits of a film one time and learnt you managed some company.'

Egg mentioned Sarah brings everything back in a dramatic flash and I suddenly feel nineteen again, seeing Sarah sitting on the wall, in her yellow top, smiling that serene smile at me. It dizzies me.

'You still talk to Sarah?'

'All the time. She lives in Nottingham.'

'How's she doing?'

Egg looks at me, 'she's married, two kids. Taryn and Cassidy.'

'Wow.' Has that much life passed between us? Have we travelled so far that nothing that was matters now? 'Pass on my congratulations.'

'So what about you Will? Are you married? Tell me what's new.'

'I'm not married, no kids. I work a lot.' You are right Will. None of this matters. What am I doing, still entertaining this conversation? 'Look, it was good to see you, but… and I don't mean to be rude… but I kind of want some time on my own.'

'Hey, hey, don't worry about it. It's not like we were ever truly friends. I said hello, we caught up, the end.' She stands and begins to walk away. I exhale deeply. Then she turns around, 'just one more thing. Sarah never meant to do what she did. She never meant to hurt you.'

Egg is still standing beside my table, looking at my bemused expression, awaiting some reaction. I look at her, at her dreadlocked hair, her porcelain face and at the sunken, hollow eyes skirting around.

'Why tell me that?' I ask. 'All that's so long ago now.'

She sits. 'She always wanted to tell you and I stopped her.' Egg picks up the menu and begins to scan the page. 'Everything's so expensive in here.'

'My treat.' I wish that she would get to the point so I can be in peace again.

'You were always a kind man. Sarah liked that about you. I'll just have a coffee.'

'Are you sure you don't want anything else?'

'A plate of chips might be good. And a bit of cake.'

I order her meal and drink, and she sits in silence for a while, playing with a strand of hair. As she does I look at her and see the changes pockmarked in her skin. There is a small scar above her right eye which I do not recall from those days at university, and though I am not sure, there seem to be needle marks on her arm. For a moment I wonder about saying something to her, about asking if there is anything I can do to help her, but in my stomach I feel something foul moving that says she is on skid-row and that this is just begging, that I am just someone with whom she has a connection and can plunder for scraps.

'Tell me about Sarah,' I say, trying to reopen the stagnant conversation.

'I told you about the kids, yeah?' I nod my head. 'She works for a lawyer, receptionist or something, I'm not really sure.'

'Does she still sing?'

'Only in karaoke. You know what her mother was against it; singing was never a career for a woman. No matter what Sarah said, she never listened. Look at Joan Baez, Rickie Lee Jones, and Joni Mitchell. That's what she'd say, and her mother would just say no.'

'I didn't think Sarah listened to what her mother said.'

'She told you that, wanted to appear independent for you. She really liked you, you know. I don't think you realise how lucky you were to have her.'

'I knew how lucky I was Egg. Don't think I didn't. I saw the way other men looked at her; I know we made mistakes, that we still had a chance. But it's ancient history now.'

Egg looks down at the table cloth as a waitress places the bowl of chips in front of her, and when the waitress asks if she wants any sauce Egg just shakes her head, as if asking for something might be a crime. She wolfs down the food, not speaking, not even really aware of my presence, it seems, until she looks up again, and with a mouthful of food asks, 'Are you with anybody now?'

'I've just separated from someone.' I lie again. I do not want her knowing of Laura. 'I don't want to talk about it. What about you, any lucky fellow in your life?'

Egg suddenly laughs, very loudly, her head tipping back, revealing her blackened, nicotine stained teeth. She looks like a clichéd tramp. I almost expect to see plastic bags around her feet. 'You never really got anything did you Will Hargreaves?

Always too busy looking at Sarah to see what was going on around you.'

'What's that mean?'

'Thanks for the food Will, at least your generosity was never at fault.' Egg stands and begins to walk away. I take a sip of coffee and look at her, 'just one more thing Will.'

'Yes?'

'I couldn't borrow a tenner?'

3.

As I walk through the city streets, lonely amongst the crowds swelling past me, I feel my mobile phone vibrating. I take it out and look at the name flashing on the screen. David's name is there, and I contemplate for a second or two about answering. I wonder what he could want with me – whether it is a business call or a personal contact. Before I can decide to answer it he rings off.

Looking around the buildings I begin to question why I am here. About what has bought me to Cambridge on this day, at this moment in time? Whether what has occurred is fated – that I was suppose to come on this day to meet Egg, so she could tell some truths about a girl I'd loved, so she could confuse my mind, and worry my heart. Sarah no longer mattered; she had stopped being of importance years ago. Laura was where my loyalties lay now; it is her that I should be thinking of, it is her that I should be talking with. In my mind's eye I see the envelope, her letter, unopened on my desk back at home. She wishes to talk. I can feel the fight with my pride and my consciousness, and the fight inside of me, in my lungs. Then the mobile phone begins to vibrate once more. Laura's name is on the screen.

The number fades as I stand there working out whether to answer. I look around the Cambridge streets, at the thousands of faces passing by, at the sun arching over the spires of the ornate architecture, and then I throw the mobile phone into a nearby bin and walk away.

There are a couple of other passengers on this night coach to Aberdeen. After throwing my mobile phone into the bin, I carried on walking the city streets, looking for something, though I knew not what, when I saw the sign advertising a cheap coach ride, and thinking not of my belongings in the hotel, or my car parked nearby, I bought a ticket.

The lights aboard are dimmed, and up in front I can see one elderly passenger reading a novel. His glasses are thin-framed, perching precariously on the end of his nose. His white hair is wispy, weather-lines stretch around his cheeks and neck. I look at this man, wonder where he is going, what his final destination is, whether he is happy or saddened, if this trip is pleasure or not. For a moment I think about asking him, and as I do I see myself like him, years from now, and wonder what I could be doing. Then I feel the cancer moving in my chest, and close my eyes, and try and answer the questions I want to ask him, for myself. Where am I going? What is my final destination? And then I think of Laura, as the strangeness of a dream pulls me under.

Just past Edinburgh I alight the coach. The driver threw up some protestations, that there was no hotel near this place, that there was nothing here but countryside. I told him that this was the place I needed, and he said 'Your funeral son,' and I couldn't help but laugh. As the red tail lights of the coach faded into the night, I began to walk along the road until I found a stile and crossing over onto the moorland I began to walk, the light of the star and the moon illuminating my path. Somehow this journey was beginning to feel right, that this was ordained, written somewhere long ago, in some forgotten book.

PART SEVEN

THE ENDING
1999

1.

Dr. Rajiv Patel sits opposite me. He is reading my case notes, the ochre file on the desk spilling out with test results, notes, and diagnoses. He takes an x-ray from the file and holds it up to the light. He expels a noise, something approximating curiosity laced with concern. The x-ray is replaced and he takes a silver pen from a penholder and writes something down. Picks up the x-ray again and has another look. "This is good." He says. "Very good." He is speaking to himself, oblivious to my presence in the seat opposite. With the pen he writes something else and then spins around in his chair to face the reference shelf behind him, sagging under the weight of such heavy texts.

As I wait for him to pronounce my fate, offer the possibilities of what might be next, I find myself thinking about Laura. We have picked a day now, a date not too far into the future that – if this cancer proves resilient, a bitter malignant pill, it is a date we both felt might be feasible. Six weeks. In six weeks I am to be married. As is the way with life, when there are urgent preparations to be made, other problems arise. When I'm not planning to wed, I'm trying to work, busy now with the news that Brad Pitt is going to be in one of our movies and so we have become swamped with finance meetings, strategic meetings, agent meetings, casting meetings, directorial meetings, script meetings, read-through meetings. The behemoth that is Riverbank Films is turning slowly in the water, aiming for richer waters. This is, we all feel, about to be our biggest break, our shot at the premier league, and we've all invested so much time and effort into it – these are my best friends, my future, the way we raise money for our children – that we have to focus more on it than our immediate life. That, under any other circumstances, I might have felt unforgiveable, but in present circumstances, in these days of doubt and worry, it is good to be thinking so far ahead, of such future plans. At night, as we sleep, I can feel Laura shake with excitement. Despite the growth inside of me, these are glorious days.

Rajiv Patel has that expression. He has not worn it since last Christmas when he told me my mother was dying.

'How bad?' I ask, already knowing the answer. It really can be the only answer. I'm sure this is fate.

'The cancer is spreading.'

'How long?'

'It's not an exact science Will.'

'How long?'

'Soon,' he says, 'soon.'

'Until I die?'

Rajiv reaches over his desk and picks up the computer keyboard. He taps a few buttons. 'You need to clear all next week Will. We need to operate. We do this now we still have a chance to excise the cancer. It is spreading, I don't like its speed, but we can stop it, abate it. You need more chemotherapy, and you will get a lot weaker.'

'I'm getting married in six weeks.'

Rajiv reaches across the desk. 'Congratulations.' We shake hands. 'You'll be holding the ceremony in the hospital.' Rajiv

216

types something into the computer. 'Right you're booked in. You need to know Will that this will not be easy. You are going to be in more pain and you will suffer. But you can beat this cancer Will. You can.'

I call Laura from outside, leaning back against a wall, watching paramedics unloading a patient on a gurney. Two doctors come running out and they wheel the man in quickly. As her number rings I wonder who that patient was, what happened to him to require such urgent medical attention. The two paramedics get back into the ambulance and drive off. I also wonder how those men cope. What mechanisms in their brains must be switched off to not become involved?

'How was it?' Laura asks.

I inform her of Doctor Patel's comments, recommendations, and plans for me. She listens attentively, and at the end of my monologue I hear her exhaling her worry.

'So it is good news. Better news anyway. Are you sure you don't need me to come pick you up?'

I tell her I am fine. 'I love you Laura.'

'I love you too.'

We hang up and I walk across the car park, towards the person that is waiting there for me. David is out of his car, on his mobile phone. He ends the call as he sees me, comes over and embraces me.

'So how was it?'

'I'm not dying so that's something.'

'But you are ill.'

'Very. I'm scared David. I'm really so scared.'

My best friend pulls me into a tighter hug and I feel myself starting to cry. We stay like that for a while as people glance at us, make assumptions about us. I'm not sure when we arrive back at my house, but we do, and David helps me up the steps. Laura opens the door.

'David called me.' She explains why she is here and not at work.

I have no memory of him calling her. I collapse into my fiancée's arms and she and David carry me into the living room where I fall onto the seat. Laura leans down beside me, kisses me. 'You don't need to protect me from how bad this is Will. I know you think you do, and that you always try to. I know this is bad. And I'm with you. I will always be with you.'

And that is enough.

2.

Tia arrives with her husband-to-be Brian, and Dad. Tia has bought flowers, Dad has the card, and Brian the grapes.

'I know it's a cliché,' Tia hugs me, 'but there you go.'

It is Dad's turn to hug me now. It is him I worry the most about. It cannot be good for his heart to see first his wife and now his son in a bed like this, with this illness. 'Tia picked out the card. Can't say I approve,' he explains, as I open it and see pictures of semi-nude women and the punch line for the joke, 'but the sentiments the important thing.'

I pass Laura the card and she reads it, groans at the joke. 'Is this really the best they can do?'

'You should have seen the other ones,' Brian says, putting the grapes on the bedside cabinet, next to the other grapes bought by other guests. By the end of this I don't think I'll ever want to see or eat another grape.

David reads the card next. 'Straight men and their fixations.' He laughs.

Though I am weakened after the therapy, the surgery to remove the cancerous growth, the constant throb of frustration, anger and fear, I have my family with me, this extended family of mine, and it is good, it works for me. Just to have them in the room it feels like someone has opened a window and a light breeze has come and blown away the pain. Laura holds my hand as Tia and Brian tell us about their wedding plans.

'And the last thing,' Tia smiles widely, looks at Brian, at me, at Dad, 'I'm pregnant.'

And all of a sudden we are not in a hospital bedroom, I'm not ill, we're somewhere else. Life is amazing.

3.

'Tell me where you went?' Laura asks.

It is the only thing of which we have not spoken. So much happened so quickly it blindsided us both. And I was stupid. I realise now how stupid I was. I did what I always had done; it was my programmed reflex, my cowardly answer to life's problems. Run. Run quickly and do not look back. I have become aware of it, aware of why the things I have remembered are important, for they were lessons I was supposed to learn. I ran from Ellie when she offered me a kiss because I feared it. I ran from Sarah in Devon because I feared what might come next if we repaired our relationship. I ran from Sarah again in the nightclub because I feared being in that relationship, I wanted the one I knew was doomed, that casual meaningless fling with Liz. And I ran from Laura, not once, but twice. I made her leave my home because I feared being in that place – being loved - though I was already there, with love embracing me – that is the irrationality of fear – and I ran, far away, when faced with the possibility of my death. Why have I always run when I know what it is I should be doing? I should be facing up to myself.

'I went to find myself.' I tell Laura, but that is not what she wants to know. She wants to know the physical details, the minutiae, because she loves me and these things matter. 'I went to Cambridge first and it was there I threw away my mobile. God knows why we do such stupid things. I met an old university friend and she, unwittingly, imparted a few home truths. And still, like the bloody fool I sometimes am, I ran away. I went to Scotland, got lost, and walked the mountains. I was an idiot Laura. I should have been here with you, not freezing myself in the middle of nowhere. I'm not running again Laura. I promise you that. This time I'm staying right here, right next to you.'

Laura kisses me. 'You better. This is our honeymoon.'

I touch her belly, swollen now, filled with emerging life. I kiss her there and listen for the heartbeat.

This is how it ends.

They are all around my bed now. Every single one of them. I look at their faces. Tia, Brian, David, Dad, and Laura. Rajiv stands a little way behind them. Around my bed are flowers, cards – from other friends, distant relatives, even some of the actors that have worked in our films, other work colleagues, writers, even the waiter from the restaurant I first visited with Laura, and where I have returned often since.

I am weak. My strength is failing, but I do not feel it. Strangely I feel most alive. Laura holds my hand. She is wearing a beautiful blue dress, and the future is etched in her body.

The priest enters the room now, his head lowered, and he begins to read a passage from the bible. Tia dabs the tears from her eyes.

'Laura Dawn Johnson do you take William Anthony Hargreaves as your husband?'

'I do.'

'And do you William Anthony Hargreaves take Laura Dawn Johnson as your wife?'

'I do.'

Tia passes the ring and I slide it onto Laura's finger.

'You may kiss the bride.'

Laura leans down and kisses me gently. Her kiss feels as electric, as passionate, as needed as the first time she kissed me, all those years ago now, back in those days when this was not even a glimmer of reality, when this was a distant dream. Her lips taste like strawberry.

The sea washes against the beach, the sun beats down on the earth with beauty and warmth. The sand feels sensual as it slips between my toes, as soft as the skin of my lover. The sea invites me in, its undulation whispering quiet words in my mind. I step into the water, and it is warm, feeling natural on my body. Its power forces memory rushing to the fore, bringing everything into focus, the present, the past and the future. I can see Tia standing on the beach in St. Lucia, next to her husband, with Dad, David and Laura next to them. I am beside my sister, holding the ring that she will in a moment be wearing on her finger. They have done it the other way round. Noisily, playing in the sand is their child, Isabelle, playing with Natalie and Casey William, my first child. The first child of many that will come afterward, in another story.

For now it is the sound of laughter, of love being confirmed, and play. It has been a long journey, from there to here, but I have made it. And as I look at my family, becoming larger still, I can only smile. I watch Casey William play and wonder what he will inherit from us; if in thirty years he will look back at this moment on the beach and see that it is the beginning of where life goes right.

Laura comes to my side.

'Hello husband.'

'Hello wife.'

'Dad's got the kids under control.' I glance at my father, digging in the sand with the kids. 'Fancy going back to the hotel room, see if we can't work on child number three?'

Yes. This is the life.

This is how my story begins.

April 2004 – Oct 2008

About The Author

Ben Dutton was born in 1979. He is a graduate of the University of Wales Lampeter, where he completed a Masters Degree in Creative Writing in 2006 and is currently studying for a PhD in the same subject. He has taught undergraduate creative writing at numerous institutions and been a lifelong supporter of creative writing circles. In his spare time he enjoys working.

The Inheritance of Things Past is his first novel, and he has already completed his second. He is currently seeking literary representation and a full publishing deal. He can be contacted on:

benjdutton@googlemail.com

Thanks

I would like to thank Dic Edwards for his continued support and mentoring, to the University of Wales Lampeter for granting me the experiences it did, and to Bob Gillham for excellent friendship and honest critiquing of my work. You've been an excellent first reader.

Also my love to my family, whose patience in face of my untiring self-belief, will finally be rewarded.

To my friends: I thank you for your support, especially Alexander Staniforth and Nicci, for their debates and friendship (and for helping me decide a crucial scene in this work). See you all in the next book.

Photographic Credit

Cover Photographs Evan Welsch "Grassy Dreams" courtesy of http://www.sxc.hu

Printed in the United Kingdom
by Lightning Source UK Ltd.
136175UK00002B/22-30/P